T0156663

A PROBABLE COMPLEX FUTURE EVOLVING FROM A HISTORICAL PAST SEEN FROM A MODERATE PERSPECTIVE

Survival of a "Sugar Daddy" vs a "Sugar Mommy"

Lux, Veritas et Vitae

Dr. Angell de la Sierra, Esq.

Order this book online at www.trafford.com
or email orders@trafford.com

Most Trafford titles are also available at major online book retailers.

Print information available on the last page.

ISBN: 978-1-4907-9171-5 (sc)
ISBN: 978-1-4907-9173-9 (e)

Trafford rev. 10/20/2018

North America & international
toll-free: 1 888 232 4444 (USA & Canada)
fax: 812 355 4082

CHAPTER 1

This is an autobiographical novel, a veridical, but fictionalized, account based on memoirs from the temporal evolution of a premature, mixed-breed orphan sharing an old house with six other cousins in Colonial Puerto Rico, life in Europe and Eastern USA.

Sorry, but this is not the narrative of a great philosopher or mathematician who has played any substantive role in the development of biophysical chemistry, medicine or law notwithstanding having been involved in their lifetime teaching, research and speculation, albeit not always by choice.

What is this all about then? In general, it is about my human unconscious survival emotions, their correlated, existential and conscious feelings and my individualized, self-conscious effort to rationalize my intuitions and speculations about the necessary and/ or convenient presence of all invisible objects or events beyond my sensory perception effort to describe or conceptual complexity to explain.

More specifically, and to my own surprise, I never suspected I would be so strongly convinced about the cognoscitive superiority of women surviving in 'macho' or 'sharia law' societies. Likewise, having grown up under the protective influence of my dear uncle Agustin Bobonis de-la-Sierra -a card-carrying Communist, Mason/Catholic, labor organizer and self-taught genius- my life hero,

I never suspected I would be now defending the existence of a Supreme but un-natural Intelligent Design/plan by using mathematical logic tools and, of course, my Christian faith. Ever since I discontinued my theology studies to become a Catholic priest at St. Meinrad Seminary in Indiana under the strong influence of Jesuits and their sometimes-controversial theology. Consequently, do not expect miracles from this biased narrative of my never ending journey towards an understanding of life and consciousness, a sort of Neoplatonic realism goal. (https://en.wikipedia.org/wiki/Platonic_realism) trying to harmonize both the reality that is imperceptible yet intelligible and the reality that is perceptible yet unintelligible considering both the perceptual and cognoscitive limitations of the human species and thus introducing the necessity of yet another variable, an un-natural theosophy. This approach hopes to harmonize the objective with the subjective, the perceptual with the conceptual and the rational with the emotional intuitions. I grew up and had remained a moderate who reacted to being confined to any restrictive/exclusive 'nominalist', non-transcendental doctrine of existential reality. Since it is impossible to think and narrate from a 'tabula rasa' frame of mind, Beware, I will not deliberately avoid any self-serving fiction to amuse myself and others.

This detailed narrative is all summarized in my "Treatise on the Neurophilosophy of Consciousness." http://delasierra-sheffer.net/home.html / Penguin Books/Trafford Inc. Publisher

EARLY CHILDHOOD INTROVERSION

I was prematurely-born a Piscean orphan near the end of the first third of the 20th. Century as an American Citizen at Presbyterian Hospital in Condado area of San Juan, Puerto Rico; right in front of that vast, tropical Atlantic Ocean bathing the shores of San Juan, the Capital of. the most beautiful of all-American colonies, Puerto Rico, the 'Pearl of the Caribbean'. Far from being born a wealthy aristocrat orphan from a renowned political monarchy, we were a middle-class family of seven children, my uncle and aunt. I was living as a supernumerary inside a big family in a small, century old house, influenced my eventual progression as an introvert, especially when my uncle singled me out when he was early impressed by my curiosity and love for learning.

We had a sash and door business plus other members of the family designed and built ornamental iron gates and fences. My uncle was very attached to his Corsican-derived two brothers and one sister who died prematurely to give me life, always very proud of their Mediterranean connections. The two brothers were well educated members of that Bobonis family of yesteryears. Attorney Cesar Bobonis was a well-known judge and Professor Dr. Augusto Bobonis was a controversial Dean of Pedagogy at the University of Puerto Rico main

Rio Piedras Campus. He taught a course in Communism that caused both of us problems with the colonial ruling party in P.R. at the time and its leader Luis Munoz Marin. In my case in 1954, when I had been accepted to start Medical School training at Temple U. and Northwestern U. after graduating from college with Honors at the University, the UPR School of Medicine had placed me only on a 'waiting list' to politically embarrass me and my family. That was too embarrassing for me to stomach.

That's the time when I became a voluntary exile in New York City from P.R. by choice. Any good university student knows that all territories aspire to be independent, especially if it has natural resources to subsist and be competitive in the market of goods and services. But P.R. only had excellent human resources, like becoming the Big Pharma developing center globally proved, but otherwise it could become a Banana Republic. But the Colonial Party solution was to invent a 'Commonwealth' status, a colony with a long leash! This way I became a Nomad in the big Apple, an angry exile by choice. As it turned out later-on I returned to the same Medical School in P.R. as a professor, the same one who had me in a 'waiting list' before!. The military and the Jewish Academia had significant roles to play in this outcome. Meanwhile, I had become both accepted at Albert Einstein School of Medicine and St. John's University during my stay in New York

EARLY EXPERIENCES IN THE COLONIAL ENVIRONMENT.

As is common to introverts, I spent many, long preteen hours daydreaming while getting sunburned –'Bajo un Palmar'-when meditatively staring at the tall palm trees laden with beautiful greenish/yellow coconuts growing way up above the white sandy beach, right in front of Ocean Park's view of the distant Atlantic Ocean reefs. What else was there to do in the quaint 'Loiza St.' village of Santurce, P.R. of the 1930's? No cell phones, tablets, television or computers to socially isolate you from interpersonal contacts with your peers. But somehow, I always managed to spend lonely hours playing with a Galen stone radio signal originating from local radio stations. The challenge was to improve the quality of the sound signal reception. Working together with Ramon Fortunno, another kid living at Flores St., a walking distance from Maria Moczo St. where I lived with eight others. With the use of a copper wire coil we managed to get radio signals from 2 or 3 stations by changing the position of a tuning needle on the surface of the cylindrical coil! At that time my family had the only radio in our mixed socio-economic neighborhood.

Pedro Geronimo Goyco was the only public elementary school within walking distance of the 'Loiza St.' villagers. There were only a few Certified Kinder and pre-Kinder schools in the area. It is never too late to tell your family now how young Yogi (me) felt during those trying days inside the 'Big Apple' metropolis and how, after my loving Irish Catholic wife of 45+ years died and how I remarried Suzy, the beautiful model and Southern Baptist Deaconess, an unintended victim of my unrelenting frustration with my life and politics. I am sorry Judy, wherever you are in heavens or elsewhere alive.

https://www.facebook.com/photo.php?fbid=10216212889981382&set=gm.10159 834636970089&type=3 Human Brain Anatomy

HOW TO SUBLIMATE GRIEVING PAINFUL EMOTIONS INTO CREATIVE EXPERIENCES.

CHAPTER

2

Dear Daniel, Barbie, Nini, Suzi and family you are about to read about a Rambling Chaos of Digressions to follow. Bear with me, just bragging a little, crying a lot as I continue to fight my chronic depression and grief. Dear family. There is not an awful lot you don't already know about the circumstances of my life, but there are a few that really made a difference, which you are yet unacquainted with, those that were part of my upbringing experiences in Puerto Rico (Macondo, USA), Spain and New York. They have forever shaped my character by providing axiological insights and various relevant perspectives to choose from as my guiding torch into the uncertainties of an always uncertain future. No, it is not either about little made-up anecdotes of my ancestors, who the hell cares about who or where they originated from, Spain, African Moors, Corsica, the Arawak Colombian Indians, Barcelona or what have you. Really, who cares? Neither is it about the relative intellectual poverty and social obscurity into which I was born and bred when my mother died after giving birth nor is it about the eventual transition upon retirement from Academia to a more leisurely lake-front retirement comfort trying to share with others in cyberspace what God and my sheltered conservative upbringing had given me. For what God has especially given to you is not meant exclusively for self-indulgence but to improve the world you found according to your guiding religious faith and your faculties, those innate or acquired. And, of course, according to your luck! I don't know if my relative successes in the HiQ world is worth sharing with others or even fit to be adopted by others under similar circumstances. Maybe so. If given an opportunity to reincarnate after my death, would I reenact the same life style and strategy patterns? I am sure I wouldn't be so lucky, given the same existential circumstances I have had to cope with, including the untimely death of my uncle, first wife and my two oldest boys. In retrospect I never expected any reward I hadn't earned by hard work and careful introspective meditation. That lesson I learned early on from Uncle Agustin Bobonis-Sierra (de la Sierra) who claimed and inherited my immature infant body soon after my mother's death, and has guided my steps throughout my entire life. He must have been crazy to add me to his other six youngens he had to feed and raise but the die was cast. He was put in my life for me to learn and follow his steps after he died while I was still in high school, a loss I will never recover from. I have been so lucky and blessed that I wouldn't have significantly changed gears or correct any major judgments on my spouse(s), children, neighbors or pets, for life is all about love and needs first and not un-affordable conveniences in that order. Stoic, sad, antisocial, shy introvert, ultrasensitive, witty, moderate, down to earth . . ., yes all of those things some loved or felt sorry about, for I never had enemies. The only thing I have missed is not being able to professionally play the piano or conduct a symphony orchestra. Someday I hope to explain the neurological details of experiencing that quale. Today I live dying, trying to understand, with tears cascading down my cheeks, why God chose me to experience the untimely death of my two oldest sons. I keep looking deeper and deeper into the complexities of neurodynamics for an explanation but to no avail. But here is Suzi, my good looking wife, to provide that motherly shoulder for me to incline my head on and dry my tears while our household zoo of dogs, cats, cranes, egrets, blue jays and buzzards, watch in awe both from the porch inside and the lake flora outside.

CHAPTER

3

If the reader didn't get bored with the tiresome account in the introduction, I will be surprised. Who listens to an old man talking to himself and his claimed achievements in front of a mirror, a soliloquy of sorts inspired mostly by vanity and self-serving indulgence? Such are the pleasures of a vanishing, lonely old life in the prelude of an obligatory transmigration and transfiguration into the unknown yonder, the same pleasure that often resulted in productive abstractions in the past. This is a sort of creative vanity that leads you to challenge and control the impossible and the invisible. It empowers you to wrestle complexity down to symbolic or sentential logical representations you hope to communicate intelligibly to reveal their inner structural/ functional secrets. Life is an illusion and illusions are just that . . ., illusions. Perhaps I was influenced by the many worthy and inconclusive projects my upbringing family experienced and now wished me to complete. On my uncle and mother's side, the Bobonis transplants from Corsica had played an important role in the founding of Carolina, then a palm tree haven in mid northern coastal Puerto Rico. There are many such Corsicans, now mostly headquartered in the southwestern tip of the island who could have participated in the development maybe, but they didn't. Instead they preferred to claim a special status because of their ethnic Sub-European/ Mediterranean origins, where Napoleon was born, tribal things that can only flourish in modern colonial Macondos where Indian aborigines and African slaves are still looked down upon. Many other Bobonis in the family became lawyers, professors, physicians and dentists we were all so proud of, but none like my dear uncle Agustin, who with only a high school diploma and an insatiable lust for books and knowledge no one could match, influenced my imagination. He was, is, and will always be my hero because when you combine natural intelligence and knowledge with honesty, humility, drive and high morals, nothing can destroy you. I only wish I could feel the same way about my good and handsome father's European side of the family whose push genes didn't match their own high morals and intelligence. When God gives us such wonderful gifts, we are automatically morally committed to push and improve the world we found, we have to . . . . The most remarkable influence that dwells deep inside my mind up to this date was my uncle's claim that he was a 'free thinker', not for sale! No wonder he was simultaneously a Catholic, a Communist, a Mason, a spiritualist, wood carving artist and a tall, good-looking labor organizer, not to mention his claim as a descendant of the French "Borbones" dynasty (via the Mediterranean Corsica). He trusted me without conditions. Somehow he felt I'd follow his advices and I sure did. He lavished me with praise when I designed my first Galen radio, able to select from different radio station frequencies from a partitioned copper coil and a rotating tooth brush frequency selector design.

Leonore Mohler and Olga Iris de Leon in grammar school were my favorite girl-friends when the term meant just that, no touching allowed, and my uncle just smiled knowingly when told about my subconscious preferences during grammar school.

CHAPTER

4

Don Juan, my tall handsome father with big rabbit ears, had buried his first American (European illegal?) wife leaving their only two children stranded between New York and Philadelphia. Whether he had originally landed in New York from Spain or Bayamon, Puerto Rico was a mystery to me since I was assiduously and deliberately kept uninformed or misinformed by all about that side of the family . . . to this day! That includes my brilliant sister Virginia, the 5-year-old precocious toddler whom my good father kept all for himself while I, a premature baby, was taken to my uncle's house for care and raising, along with their other six children.

My uncle's century-old house was not far from the infinite north Atlantic Ocean, that blue wavy vastness that witnessed so many of my dreamy preadolescent moments while lying down on the white sandy beaches, staring at the green coconuts hanging high from the tall palm trees. I scorched under the tropical sun that turned my face color to a lobster shade and my hair to look like a matted bleached rope. A Piscean by birth, I had developed a strong liking for the sea; what else was there to do after working the post school afternoons in my Uncle's wood shop? After that we had supper and was then given a thick book to spend the early evenings reading—by the kerosene lamp—about the Marxist Revolution as seen by the Red Dean of Canterbury, England, the classic "The Soviet Power". I had also learned early to swim well, snorkel, and manage small canoes with Cecil and Cheo Nater and other neighborhood boys. I was never seen nor felt like a leader among my friends. I was lonely, sad, and dejected. Only once in a lifetime did I have a fist fight with anyone. It was a reflex response to the neighborhood's bully, Jose Manuel (Chepo) Costoso, who once noticed I was concealing a handful of coins inside my closed fist and carrying a loaf of bread under the other arm's pits when returning home from my quotidian trip back from the bakery. He asked me 'cleverly' what I was carrying inside my closed fist. As I was getting ready to innocently raise my arm, open my closed fist and show him, he whip-slapped my closed hand causing the coins to scatter on the pavement. My response reaction peaked after my frightened attempt to recover the coins, an unexpected turn of events. In retrospect, it is a recurring memory how I was driven blindly to survive my anticipated beating by repeatedly hitting Chepo Costoso again and again in fear. He never bothered me again. Every time I left the house heading to main street, Loiza Street, to shop or catch a bus, I could feel the many watchful eyes of my sister-cousins behind me following my slow steps to the corner street before I turned. I felt loved and protected, God bless my cousins Ana, Sixta and Susana.

There is still a deep-water submerged canyon area near a wharf, 'El Ultimo Trolley', where sometimes, on week-ends, I used to practice deep sea diving with a home-made pointed iron rod spear attached by its rounded end to a length of rubber from an old Firestone rubber inner-tube. My diving friends and I caught small marine life with the sharp spear which probably may have dissuaded Chepo, the bully, from getting too close to me? Besides, I had an athletic build, a muscular 5'6" middle stature, the result of sand papering at my Uncle's shop, weight lifting, and soccer playing exercise. That contrasted with my other personality side as a classic music collector with Benjamin Curet Cuevas, the minister's son. Once in High School I also enjoyed painting and choir singing and, all of it done quietly without ever saying too many words about it to anyone, an introvert style many still think characterizes my demeanor. This acquired attitude no doubt results from the daily lessons received about the hierarchy of values where needs come ahead of conveniences, where the content of books or people deserve more attention than the dress or book cover, where axiological considerations always come ahead of physical satisfaction, etc.

Uncle Agustin was both a preacher and a practitioner. It was his pride that all seven of us children and his wife, Maria, lived comfortably, in good health and reputation, all earned through his hard labor, industry, honesty, and the grace of God. Once in a blue moon I would meet my shy, soft-spoken Don Juan, my biological father, who dropped by for a short social visit to exchange pleasantries and random chatting. As our hearts readied to bond, we were always interrupted after a short while. There were then no hugs as I watched his departure, teary-eyed, as he slowly left our home near the ocean and disappeared in the distance . . . It was heartbreaking, and I was always left wondering why I could not hold his hand and walk with him to his house or maybe keep him with me. Why could I not leave my uncle's home holding hands with that handsome nice man my sister Virginia possessively loved so much? Those were my first confusing lessons about life and its meanings. But, to neutralize that anguish, there was always a late afternoon when that other tall, strong, balding man that, upon returning from work, empty lunch box in hand,. he would hug me and bring stability to my quotidian life along with Ana Luisa, the oldest daughter, who cared for me and my baby needs as if I had been her own son. The circumstances whereby my father ended up in Puerto Rico from New York to marry my mother Barbara—Uncle Agustin's sister and confidante—will always remain a mystery. Everything having to do with my father was always kept a mystery. I learned recently that before he died from a gall bladder post surgical complication there was a mysterious reunion of that side of my family but I was not invited. C'est la vie . . . Later on, I finally adjusted to that circumstance and decided to quit worrying and eventually formally ('de jure') degraded his last name to a middle initial 'O.', something that had 'de facto' already happened for a long time. I still remember many, many years back when I had held my breath in vain hoping he would show up when I graduated Valedictorian with my uncle's last name 'Bobonis' from Goyco Elementary School in Santurce. The same expectation vanished at my middle school, high school and university graduations with distinctions. C'est la vie. I only had one sister, Virginia, who my uncle always reminded me that: "She has always had A's in her school record, never a B." This warning was often followed by having me learn the Spanish 28 letters of the alphabet with colored cards soon after I was able to sustain a stable erect position from crawling! I was able to read before I walked! This made possible for me to read the newspaper before I could walk a long straight line without wobbling and falling on my diaper-covered fanny. True, it took a long time for me to walk but I could read before I walked! Cool! I remember the times when I was crawling and soiled my diaper to Ana Luisa's chagrin and scolding, just like I don't remember anytime I couldn't read thereafter. Aurea, my pre-kinder teacher at Aponte Street, would routinely put me to sleep on a comfortable bed with a glass of orange juice so she could teach the other pre-kinders how to read. There were 6 other first cousins in my household to attend to and so it was hard on Tia Maria to care for me. But she found time to teach me the alphabet with the colored cards. Maybe that was the reason why, just before celebrating my 5th birthday, I was already in first grade. Because of my previous home-schooling training, I was tested and placed in 3rd grade. I was too young and instead became an assistant and errand boy to the teaching staff who would spoil me by managing my schooling as a private student until graduation. I seldom saw a structured classroom until after graduation from elementary school. This well-meant experience would forever thereafter keep me away from structured class learning, and I had to depend almost exclusively on book reading to take my exams, I couldn't follow the classic theme presentation by the teacher and consequently I was always day dreaming in the classroom when I attended classes or just cut classes a lot. If there was no text for me to read, or if no text books were assigned, I struggled to get a B or a C in future university exams based on somebody else's class notes if and when available. In retrospect, I believe my uncle was preparing me to retrace his steps in the advance of his socialist ideals, never suspecting I would—with my nascent free enterprising ideas— eventually influence his beliefs more than he could influence mine. When he once opted to open his own 'Sash and Door' business, I had the opportunity to soften-up a little his extreme liberal views. When I became, at the age of nine, a part of his employee team, a 'voluntary' worker always fascinated with everything he said, while I sand-papered doors, moldings and windows, operated light machinery, ordered wood supplies, etc. I was in an enjoyable voluntary servitude after school and Saturdays. At that same time, on Sundays, I was tied up with the activities of Santa Teresita Catholic Church and San Gabriel's Convent where catholic nuns trained the deaf mute children. I had the best of two world cosmogonies, the liberal and the conservative. I was becoming a moderate, a free thinker myself and somewhat of an idealist activist, of the shy variety.

During my early teen years I managed to publish and edit the Central High school newspaper, Vocero Centralino where, against the administration wishes even when we respectfully criticized curricula, budgets, etc. But the best part was when I would write and exchange poetry and notes with blue eyed, blond Nectar de la Rosa who could play the piano, dance like a sphinx and later-on became a psychiatrist. High school years are memorable, ping pong and soccer varsity player, French and advanced math classes, choir, etc. No distractions from cell phones or I-pods. But good things don't last long. Before the end of high school, 1950, my dear uncle Agustin died, his sweet cigar fumes and his warm, bright smile gone forever. My world collapsed and as a result, I lived in a trance and felt that I, too, had died. I entered as an honor student my freshman year at the 'State' University of Puerto Rico (UPR). But shortly before then, I had tried an escape and for that whole summer I wanted to become a Jesuit priest along with Bolivar Defendini and Valentin Rivera-Guevara at a St. Meinrad, Indiana convent. When I saw those pretty convent girls and my unconscious commitment to provide my future children the fatherly attention I never got from my own, I knew priesthood was not meant for me. Today I honestly think I have lived up to that commitment. The short Seminary sojourn did not work for me and actually only Valentin eventually became a priest. I returned back to P.R. to start UPR. With the absence of my uncle provider, I was determined to become self-sufficient. So, I had also enrolled at the National Guard 482nd Field Artillery Battalion by lying about my age. The unit was headquartered in Puerta de Tierra, near the Escambron Beach Club. When my unit was activated to fight in the Korean War, I wanted to go so badly and quench my grieving pains that I began packing some things at home. However, I was not of age and was left behind after having happily packed my military gears as well. That failed plan was devastating at that time but became an important first experience in planning. The 482nd. Field Artillery battalion and many of my buddies disappeared in action as I gravitated into my freshman university experience with the highest entrance score. Only Arcilio Alvarado and other prominent names somehow survived that stupid Korean war. As it turned out it was meant only to be followed by the subsequent monopolistic capitalism ventures of the oil cartels . . ., my uncle's predictions still resonating today as presidential elections begin. I was lost without my uncle but my dear cousins supported me, especially Sixta who will undoubtedly become a saint and Ana Luisa. I had scored 99% in the university entrance examination and was allowed to take choir, soccer Varsity training, ROTC and honor literature courses besides other formative courses totaling the 21 credit limits to distract me from the irreparable grieving of my uncle. I still miss him to this day more than 60 years later, but I know he is up there at Antares, that bright spot on the tail of the constellation Scorpio. When I felt lonely, I could always talk to him while I rocked my chair in the dark nights on the porch at 18 Maria Moczo Street. I have memorialized my uncle and Antares in my third published volume of "Neurophilosophy of Consciousness." Back at the main Rio Piedras campus of the state university (UPR), I was always attracted to literature, classical music, and philosophy. Celinda, my next door neighbor and the first girl I ever especially noticed in my life, had disappeared along with my friend, Nectar de la Rosa, so I got busy. I started then to sublimate my grieving pain by trying to be productive in creative ways. I wrote an essay for a literature prize competition under Prof. Dr. Porras Cruz. Just like I had done in High School when I dared to report on a book read that only existed in my imagination because I had no time to read, when I finished my 'book report' on "El Vengador Escarlata." (The Scarlet Avenger) I even wondered if such existed in real time. This time at UPR, for my essay I had concocted a trip to a galaxy where my uncle was sure there would be found life. Camilo Flamarion's cosmological trips to other planets, the fight for a socialist republic, all inside the ecstasy of the tragic vibrations of Brahm's symphonies fascinated both of us. After a few weeks following submission and faculty evaluation of my essay, I was told I had won first prize . . . but, with conditions. They looked at me straight in my face and said I was supposed to visit the University psychiatrist 3 afternoons a week for tests and evaluations. I was deeply depressed with my uncle's loss, not unlike later on when I lost my beautiful Irish first wife, Judy, and more recently my two older sons. When will this agony come to an end? I cannot wait and harbor a death wish in my heart. Yet, there is so much left to do. At the psychiatrist's comfortable quarters inside UPR Rio Piedras Campus, I was subjected to a battery of tests. I had failed the arrangement of the lettered cubes and Rorschard tests but had scored at the 170+ IQ level. That meant nothing to me at that time or now, it is just a potential to develop and not a label to broadcast, socialize, and brag about as it happens now at American Mensa. At that time, still a teenager, more important were the refreshment and cookies received while comfortably resting on the psychiatrist's couch, a perfect way to end a busy afternoon in college. I became so addicted to that comfort that I feigned disorientation and stress; a strategy to continue with the afternoon sessions of brownies, refreshments and accolades. It didn't take long for the 'shrink' to catch onto my trick and booted me out of the office with an approving smile of my 'loco' acting. In a departing scene, he said I would never have problems I could not handle, "you are ok," he said with a parting smile. But I knew better that there are problems you cannot ever solve, the death of your loved ones.

CHAPTER

5

College time had been all about distraction from the vacuum created by my painful loss and of making enough money in the National Guard, setting up labs in chemistry, etc. to become self-sufficient. After that came soccer, choir, and ROTC, no time for anything else. I had practically finished all of my graduation requirements in chemistry as a 'junior' in college and during my fourth year, I became a part time assistant lab instructor in physical chemistry with Drs. Juan D. Curet and Garcia-Morin. Meanwhile, I had applied and was accepted to medical school at Chicago's Northwestern University, and Philadelphia's Temple University Medical School, all except at UPR Medical School where I was on a waiting list. As destiny would have it, later on I became one of its professors in physiology and biophysics, the kinds of political 'things' that can only happen in colonies, like Macondo, USA. Following college graduation, my libertarian disposition told me it was time for me to move on even though I felt my uncle's family welcomed me and would have preferred that I get a job and share the household company and expenses with them but destiny had different plans for me. I had to leave Macondo, USA and exile myself from the petty politics and social life in a colony of 'mantengo' philosophy. The beginnings of illegal immigration from Colombia, Cuba, and Dominican Republic had just started as soon as mainland USA extended welfare benefits to the colonials. This also caused a massive exodus of agricultural jibaritos to the city leaving the beautiful mountain harvests unattended. I left for New York with Cristino Colon, a real good friend, who weeks later returned to Puerto Rico to start medical school studies. He never understood how I had better grades and was still on a waiting list at the UPR state's medical school. However, as political gossip goes, one of my Bobonis uncles had taught Marxist philosophy at UPR University at Rio Piedras main campus, which in hindsight, I think was the problem. Even my sister, Virginia, questioned the admission committee's logic. Meanwhile, I worried from my temporary abode in Bronx, New York where I stayed with my brother-cousin Augusto. How could I afford Northwestern University Medical School in expensive Chicago or Temple University in Pennsylvania that had accepted me?. In reality, I was not sure I wanted a vocation in the medical profession where you must deal with sick people in pain showing runny, bloody, lesions and moaning as I had seen with lab animals in elementary biology which I hated. To illustrate, later on in Spain, when working at the Oncological Institute of Madrid as a research doctor on sabbatical leave from Georgetown Medical School, my beautiful first daughter, Barbara, was born. My scared wife, Judy, had already delivered 3 boys with anesthesia and the only choice available was given to me in plain Spanish, "If you want it, you can scrub and administer some pentothal yourself, just keep monitoring the vital signs." With my scared assistance to the obstetrician in charge, Dr. Botella LLusia, Barbie came into life. It then flashed into my memory what my aunt and cousins always said about my early vocations: ". . . musicians and philosophers die hungry. You have to be an engineer, a doctor or a lawyer." Life is always a compromise between conceptual dreams and perceptual realities. So be it.

After the first UPR college saga, I came back to the USA and New York for keeps, the city I had adopted, the one that saw me grow and develop as a responsible human being beginning with the co-founding of the Puerto Rican Forum to involve Hispanics in the political process. Little did they know I would end up defending workfare instead of colonial welfare and becoming a Republican with the blessing of Nelson Rockefeller. I was too proud to extend my arm begging when I could work for my sustenance instead.

I was received in Bronx, New York again by my dear cousin, Augusto. He lived there at this time with his wife and mother-in-law who didn't like me very much. They lived in tight quarters. I was too shy and broke to start making acquaintances among the young people spending time in the bars and cafes on either side of the elevated train station at Southern Boulevard, not far from White Plains. I was never a bar or a bed hopper, preferred small crowds and never talked much. Until I decided where to continue my studies, I was constantly being reminded from an Antares star above that I had to concentrate my efforts on earning money by my honesty, industry, and frugality. Without computers, e-mails, Skype, computer phones or inexpensive ways of communication at that time, I felt isolated and depressed. I had occasional contacts with my dear cousins back at Macondo, USA, but never from my father. My only friend in New York was a 60+ year old Dr. di Targiani, a philosophy professor from Fordham University, who liked chatting with me. He insisted I date Frosso Papaeugeniou, a pretty Rhodes Scholar student from Greece. I did for a while and then missed her beautiful erudite company after she had to return to Athens upon finishing her studies at Colombia University. Then I met Peter Lardis, another great Greek friend who invited me to their ocean front home at Port Jefferson, near Brookhaven Lab in Long Island. There we enjoyed diving for Long Island Sound cherry-stone clams and enjoyed Feta cheese with Huso, a powerful Greek drink. I never thought I would enjoy New York so much; Metropolitan Opera, Carnegie Hall, Guggenheim Museum, Yankee Stadium, long trips by subway at night from Southern Boulevard in the Bronx to Brooklyn and yonder, to ponder and dream. Everything was there. I loved NY and learned a lot from its people, its majesty and opportunities. I never thought my first job in New York, after being probably the first assistant chemistry lab instructor in UPR history while still a senior in college, would be pushing a cart with clothing along busy New York streets where everybody detected my Hispanic features. In colonial Macondo, USA in the 1940's, the blue-collar folks were seen with class prejudice. However, watching brilliant doctoral candidates, of all accents, skin color, sex and political affiliations serving food and washing dishes at the restaurants, it didn't take me long to overcome the Spanish 'hidalgo' cultural prejudice. I began pushing my cart with pride and making lots of money in the process—only in America! My uncle was right, as long as you do the right things and behave, what others think about you is their problem, not yours to worry about!

My lodging needs in New York took me to all the three city boroughs traveling along the famous Triboro Bridge that takes its name from its branching to Queens, Bronx and Manhattan. In none of them was I able to establish neighborly roots and lasting acquaintances. New York is in a constant state of flux and people don't get to know each other very well but always wave at you when passing by. Somehow, I always preferred old, quaint locations where everybody knew me, my family and each other, like those in Santurce, P.R. and now in Deltona, Florida. My original Bronx location was not my choice as it was for my cousin Augusto, the hospitable and talented diamond cutter. He asked me to join his family and share their small quarters. I remembered what his father, my uncle, had done for me when I was born. Charity was heritable and so I moved in with them. At the beginning, and for a while, I was always awakened by the rattle friction noise between wheels and rails of the White Plains bound train as it applied the brakes to stop at Southern Boulevard Station, not far from 'cousin' Carmen's apartment. Many insomniac nights I would leave the building and take the dime train ride south, to the end of the subway line in Brooklyn and back, now ready to sleep. The long ride gave me a perfect solace to ponder and reflect about my next move about going to study medicine or related but non-clinical research aspects. After adjusting to the inevitable, after a while, I anticipated and really needed to hear the metallic rattle of the elevated train pass, so I could fall asleep, an interesting lesson about life. I was close to City College, St. John's University, and Albert Einstein Medical School and owned an old Studebaker (the 'old lady'). The well-paid street-cart-pushing union job had ended, and I had to find a job somewhere, with live-in facilities if possible. That meant no more affordable back pack solo trips to Europe, traveling by train with no more than a medium-sized satchel. I was lucky to find work as a counselor at Irvington on the Hudson, the place of the Sleepy Hollow Ichabod Crane, and not far away from Ossining, New York where the penitentiary was located. I started my professional career as a counselor for 'Irvington House' which housed teen agers afflicted with auto-immune rheumatic fever. It was not far from the beautiful Hudson River or the rustic train station, always ready with a train going south to Grand Central Station in Manhattan. At Irvington House, I devoured book after book of anything that fell into my hands. There I met a beautiful Irish born nurse, Miss Mclooney, a devout Catholic who wanted to marry me but I was not ready. I was obsessed with carrying on my uncle's plan for me to succeed in anything by reading anything that was published anywhere.

That yearn for novelty caused me to accept a job offer as a research associate at Cornell University Medical School, Department of Surgery, located at York Avenue, the center of Yorkville, a German enclave facing the East River . . . ., a Piscean who couldn't stay away from the rivers, lakes or oceans. It was an ideal location, walking distance from Rockefeller University, Sloan-Kettering Institute (SKI), City University of New York (CUNY) and a bus ride to New York University (NYU). Drs. William Barnes and Frank Redo, my employers, were too busy with their human surgery. After learning surgical techniques used in experimental dog work they trusted me enough to carry my own research on reflux esophagitis which we published in 'Surgical Research' Journal. Meanwhile I had simultaneously completed two master-level studies at CUNY and NYU. The first CUNY thesis was done at the Biometrics Dept. of Cornell Med. School and Sloan-Kettering Institute for Cancer Research (SKI), under Dr. Melvin Schwartz, that wonderful brainy Jewish soul. It was a mathematical thesis describing the kinetics of particle/fluid transfer across body physiological compartments using partial differential equations. I finished the

Cornell-SKI program but never claimed a diploma from NYU because I was promptly hired by SKI Biophysics Dept. located in beautiful Rye, New York, bordering the Connecticut border. I had to drive north from NYC every day along the NY thruway and was wondering how long the 'old lady' Studebaker would take it. As it turned out, it was all worth it because it was there in Rye, New York where, in a Russian class, I met Judy Sheffer, a beautiful reddish-brown-haired Irish co-worker I was destined to spend almost half a century with in company of our five children. Working at SKI at Rye, NY was a blessing in disguise in many respects even though the highway driving, and the pressure were exhausting. At that time, I was offered a full scholarship for MD/PhD studies at Albert Einstein Medical School of Yeshiva University in the Bronx. I couldn't turn down the unique opportunity to live at the Abraham Mazur student residence with those brainy Jewish people I had admired and appreciated as friends. The pressure to make decisions and the hurried married life were asphyxiating me. I had to do something soon because I didn't want to leave SKI and their superb research facilities either . . . Probably based on my good grades and what was considered a good masters-level math thesis, Albert Einstein School of Medicine (Yeshiva University) confirmed their offer for honor registration in an MD/PhD program, room and board at the medical school Abraham Mazur lodging facility. I was elated. I had never met so many studious, serious-minded and religious people in my life. They were also very friendly with a Catholic like me. The medical curriculum was breath-taking but the class discussions were in-depth and I learned something new every day. I made good friends also, like with Dick Zackheim and others. I don't remember their names but I do remember a lady Israeli soldier turned medical student who became a close friend. Dick had a strange connection with the door entrance ticket man and ushers at the Metropolitan Opera House for Saturday afternoon operas. We could stand up and enjoy the whole opera for only a quarter. Dick and I had a standing argument as to who was better—Roberta Peters or Amelita Galli Curci. We and our Israeli friend, who was a good-looking red head (who is now probably a good physician back in Israel) spent hours together talking about the Middle East problems with Egypt, Jordan, Saudi Arabia and Palestine. Iran and Syria were not so prominent then. I often wonder about our friend's whereabouts now that Iran is sworn to pulverize the chosen people.

I cannot ever forget how, in the middle of medical school final exams, I was contacted and told that Don Juan, my father, had died. I could not attend his funeral because I had no money except my scholarship. My sister, to this day, has never forgiven me for being absent at the funeral. Confusion, guilt feelings, depression and lack of concentration followed. It was not as bad as when my uncle died, but the resulting problems with my sister's side of the family still linger. I did not take some exams and nearly failed others and was put on probation for the strictly clinical courses following. Then, my good luck made possible a special arrangement for the PhD end of the combined degree program. I would be allowed to do the research at the known facilities at SKI at Rye, N.Y. This time, instead of traveling to New York City after work at SKI, next time, after marriage, it would be to Long Island, via Throggs Neck bridge over the Long Island Sound, a long but pleasant drive along the 'Bunny Trail' path bordering the Long Island sound with Judy on board the Studebaker, the 'old lady'. The previous fun rides to New York City had bonded us and cemented our relationship and we decided to get married in cold wintry St. Paul, Minnesota in December 1960. After traveling by car to St. Paul, Minnesota to get married, we rented our first house in the ritzy area of Jamaica Estates, L.I., a walking distance from St. John's University main campus from where I would graduate a few years later. Judy continued working at SKI with Dr. Jacquez's cell and tissue cultures while I got very busy with Dr. Eidenoff at the SKI Biophysics lab. Judy kept working until Angell Jr. was born. She was a very supportive woman and I had maintained a good relationship with her curly, red-haired Irish mother from County Mayo, Ireland, now deceased. Her two brothers, Gene and Jim Sheffer, and I maintain our friendship to this day. In the Biophysics lab, I was given the task of designing the optimal X-ray/cortisone treatment for Sprague-Dawley rats to carry, without rejection, Rous Sarcoma tumors used variously in assays to evaluate treatment protocols of hosts carrying deadly Rous Sarcoma virus in a tumor. Dr. Eidinoff, who oversaw the lab., was a very busy University Physics Professor. He depended heavily on me to run the lab. Which I did by always being on time, being orderly and creative, besides maintaining a trouble-free lab. That soon changed when it became my PhD thesis research laboratory. I ran a smooth operation and made him unwilling to part with me when I decided to finish the research end of my agreement with Albert Einstein School of Medicine. When I talked to him about my new lodging facilities in Long Island and professional future plans, he offered me a deal I could not turn down. I could keep my full time job at Sloan Kettering and use all of the resources of the institution, including such niceties as electron microscopy, isotopes, and all kinds of biophysical and biochemical tools to work on a doctoral project SKI was interested in. I was both fascinated and scared at working out the plan alone. In addition,

I would be tracking the biophysical/biochemical changes in a normal chick embryo fibroblast in its transition/transformation to becoming a cancer cell, a sarcoma, after getting infected with Rous Sarcoma Virus. I was perplexed at the prospect of following and describing how a crystalline white powder in a test tube labeled 'RSV' could become alive, infectious, and invasive of other cells after being cultured with normal cells—Alive!! In my original report, I had called the miraculous virus nucleoprotein a truncated life which found its complement by stealing it from the normal fibroblast host cell. Life in potency had become life in act. I couldn't wait to see that moment when life was somehow insufflated into a crystalline substance, but, as destiny would have it, the virus nucleoprotein had just disappeared while many things were happening inside the cell, as described. Not even the electron microscope could track the nucleoprotein's evolutionary grand finale. At that time the genetic code, in particular, and molecular biology, in general, was still immature and the workings of m-RNA, rybosomes role, etc. were still a subject of speculation. Who would have suspected that the viral nucleoprotein had incorporated itself into the fibroblast host DNA and there to be 'copied' by transcription and the information transferred by m-RNA to serve as a template for the synthesis of an enzyme, one gene one enzyme! I missed that but not Howard Temin whose imagination had him invoke the translation of RNA virus segment information by an unknown RNA polymerase, a reverse transcription. He used some of our SKI data to win a Nobel Prize.

I was happy but disappointed and, by the time my doctoral work was finished, accepted and published, I rejected an offer to work at Seton Hall College of Medicine, Microbiology Department to further that kind of investigation. I decided to change directions and select an area of research so complex that grants would not be so competitive to obtain and fewer people to compete with. That was the nervous system. So, after finishing the complex agreement with all concerned at SKI, Yeshiva University and St. John's University, our family headed south for Washington, DC and Maryland where research money was, even when commercial computers were not available yet. Only the federal government had such computing facility and was very much in a primitive stage, people worked inside their computers . . . . Like I would also upon arrival.

CHAPTER

After what seemed like a never-ending trail from New York along New Jersey turnpike, my then family of three finally arrived at Sonoma Rd. in Bethesda, Maryland. Angell II, born in Long Island, NY, was barely an infant. The Smithsonian Institution was organizing a Science Information Exchange (SIE) and needed someone to handle the notices on research projects (NRP) on cellular and molecular biophysics funded by public tax monies. I was hired to handle the research activities at the National Institute of Health (NIH). It was fascinating having witnessed the growth of knowledge that preceded the discovery of the DNA double helix structure. My plush office was inside a huge government computer that coordinated the scientific research activities of the whole nation. We were strategically located near Georgetown University, NIH, and the nuclear energy facilities of the Armed Forces Radiobiology Research Institute (AFRRI) at National Naval Medical Center (NNMC), George Washington and American Universities. It was fun to learn computer programming in Fortran and Basic and help develop a system to facilitate the information exchange between federal grantee researchers. Under Dr. Foster, that amiable, tall gentleman from New Orleans, I personally handled the cellular and molecular biophysics "Notice of Research Proposals" (NRP), exchanges, and even published a magazine where virus researchers could express their brainstorms. I kept up to date with professional developments by attending conferences held weekly at NIH, across the street from NNMC and AFRRI. After spending much time as a desk biomedical scientist writing basic computer programs and shuffling and feeding IBM cards into the computer operational system, I began missing the laboratory. However serviceable I might still have been to the Smithsonian, I felt I was just existing and going nowhere, the 'sane psychosis' of curiosity had seized upon me. Once things got organized, my professional services would become every day of less importance, as others with less academic training could run the show for less tax-payers money. So, I became a full time military officer and part-time consultant to AFRRI whose linear accelerator (Linac) was actively producing much needed material for the raging war effort in the Vietnam peninsula. I had escaped uniformed military participation before when my 482nd. Field Artillery Battalion disappeared in combat and an unusual situation came up. I reactivated my army military commission into Air Force wings that would allow me to fly freely over so many unanswered medical and scientific issues and "do my thing." The best part of it was that I could do research in civilian clothes except for summer special training at School of Aerospace Medicine (SAM) in San Antonio, Texas or elsewhere as needed. Now I was a full-time researcher at AFRRI assigned the mission of isolating and characterizing an erythropoietic stimulating factor (ESF) found in hydrazine-stimulated animals whose plasma could be used as treatment (e.g., plasma expander) for injuries in the battle field. We induced anemia in sheep after provoking hemolysis of red cells with injectable hydrazine. I was happy I was not directly involved in such sacrifices which reminded me of the many dogs we had to sacrifice to evaluate the effects of a chemical I had isolated from gastric juice and now dissolved and dripped into animals with Barret's esophageal lesions or reflux esophagitis when at Cornell Medical School. I felt terrible about the animals but it was necessary I was told. Besides, the only other alternative for the dogs was death at the pound. I never suspected either that years later I would be using stereotaxic equipment to implant electrodes into living cat's brains to study their behavioral change upon selective electric stimulation. The results were verified by sacrificing animals and verifying the exact position of the brain electrodes. I am glad I don't have to do it anymore. It was not always a rosy path at AFRRI. I had the best equipped lab in the country, ultracentrifuge and all, and published all kinds of findings on the erythropoietic activity of the fractions isolated and purified by paper and column chromatography. However, the only catch was that the results were classified and internally published, leaving my name out and crediting it to one Dr. Sigmund Baum, my boss. When I found out and politely complained, he let me know that the military felt that once the recombination synthesis of erythropoietin was possible, my GS-13 equivalent pay was excessive, and thought I should take an abatement on the non-military end of my contract. Since I had not anticipated this development, I waited while Dr. Baum slowly grew by degrees less civil, showed boss authority which he never had before, occasionally found fault, and was ready to let me go elsewhere. Fortunately I was granted a funded faculty position at Georgetown University Medical School by NIH and allowed me to maintain a consultant position with AFRRI. In retrospect, I admit that once Dr. Marshall Nirenberg, et al had deciphered the genetic code across the street from us at NIH, it was a matter of time before genetic recombination techniques would synthesize erythropoietin in much cheaper, faster and reliable ways than the classical physical chemistry procedures I was using, as I had tried telling my boss . . . ., not that he understood what I was talking about. I tried to join the NIH team for a few hours/days to get familiar with the work going on but there were too many trying the same thing at that time. I saw it coming, and when I realized it long before it happened, I knew I had to change gears. My biophysical chemistry research, interesting as it could have been, was destined to become obsolete and I would be expendable. I thought I would try teaching 'molecular physiology' to medical and graduate students at Georgetown Medical School not so far away.

I accepted a grant from NIH to do some membrane biophysics research which I combined with my teaching. I told Dr. Baum that I would not compete with him for a position at the Armed Forces Medical School in Bethesda, Maryland, that his wish that I find an opportunity to work on the nervous system was unnecessary, for I would leave that instant and stop at Georgetown University Medical School where I already had a job waiting for me. Dr. Larry Lilienfield, Head of the Department of Physiology and Biophysics was waiting for me. To my chagrin, I later found out that Dr. Baum's offer to give me a good recommendation anywhere I went was tested only to find out he praised me but warned that I may become too independent, a free thinker, something deemed not so good in team research.

My opportunity to land an NIH group job in Puerto Rico disappeared on the warning about me being an indomitable 'free thinker', like my uncle had been. I had forgotten I was referring to life inside super political Macondo, USA.

When at Georgetown U. Medical School, I was finally doing what early on I had thought was my vocation, combining research with teaching. And I was really happy being married to Judy, that beautiful Irish red head. None of the girls were born yet but three boys kept her plenty busy in our brick house with an acre-fenced yard in Kensington, Maryland. It was not far from Rock Creek Palisades, as we discovered later-on, when water began seeping ever so slowly into our huge basement office. The pay from my NIH grant and basic faculty salary was not bad and allowed me to gradually pay off the debts I owed for my successful allergy desensitization and constant billings from the pediatricians.

Things were looking up but, like my uncle would say, "Always secure your credit and character as a serious-minded person, be truthful and always make your word and last name your best assets." I took care not only to be industrious and frugal, but to avoid all appearances to the contrary, and I made sure I never caused scandal and paid duly for what I bought. I can say today that I can die in peace knowing that all of my children were transmitted and assimilated the same principles of Christianity and fair play. It helped that nowhere in sight were places of idle diversion. It is true that we never went out golfing, fishing or shooting because our three boys were too small and Romeo, our huge Great Dane filled our hearts. A fellow professor from Georgetown sold us a cat to keep Romeo company, but the cat turned out to be crazy and we had to return it. Romeo was relieved. Angell Jr. was overactive inside and outside his crib and sometimes pounded on his brothers, Johnny and Daniel. Who could have known that many years later that six foot six inch, 200+ pound Navy electronics expert son would be confined to a wheel chair depending heavily on both of them? At Georgetown Medical School, things were developing slowly. My course in 'Molecular Physiology and Biophysics' was too biophysically oriented to attract many graduate students and even less medical students as electives.

I joined one, Dr. Allen, in developing a bioelectric cell. He used chemical solutions, but I was more familiar with the cellular monolayers growing on a glass surface like the ones I had used when at SKI. The glass was now replaced with a platinum electrode surface and connected to a voltage recording apparatus to measure the current output and power generated as the cells grew inside an experimental, special media.

Later on, I would present my results at the Biophysical Society Congress in Moscow and Mexico where I was received royally. In the middle of the cold war, when I arrived in Moscow, I was assigned an academic escort/interpreter. I did not know Russian enough to carry a conversation, ditto for my escort in English nor Spanish so we settled for "Pig German" and plenty of body language. Wonderfully, I was able to attend the opera house to watch an unbelievable ballet performance of Tchaikovsky's "Swan Lake." I also attended mass, where Eastern ritual was not unlike the Catholic equivalent I was used to in the west. To my surprise, I was invited to fly to Akadem Gorodoff, (City of the Academy), Siberia where all eastern important research was done. There I did three unforgettable things: Placed my signature on a special library book, collected stones along the shores of the largest existing Lake Baikal, and made a long-distance call to my wife, Judy, on the other side of the world. Angell Jr.

received a shoe box full of the beautiful stones as a present. I realized that I did not feel satisfaction doing such bioelectricity research because while I was becoming more sophisticated with the various academic disciplines I had to be familiar with, I saw no marketable practical application in sight. I knew that soon the NIH funding would be revised and I would have to again shift gears.

I received an opportunity to get a sabbatical license and was invited to work at the Oncologic Institute in Madrid, Spain. I combined my experience at SKI and Georgetown and would try growing rapidly-dividing cancer cells on Platinum electrodes. By doing so, I could either increase the output of the bioelectric cell and/or learn more about the mysteries of the cancer cells, the same ones that years later took the life of my dear Judy to heaven.

So, on to Madrid with wife and three boys . . . The airplane trip to Madrid from Dulles Airport in Washington, DC took more than 13 hours traveling with the three boys and a TV set which I kept under the airplane seat. It was a nightmare trying to control toddler Angell Jr. Everybody was happy when the airplane landed at Barajas Airport outside Madrid. We were supposed to stay for a few days lodging at a motel until contact was made with the Oncological Institute. After an overnight stay with Angell Jr. antics, we were told it would be in everybody's best interests if we left the motel. With the help of an employee of University of Madrid Medical School, we secured a nice fifth floor apartment on the road to Asturias, near Madrid. We spent many nights trying to keep Angell Jr. from the windows and wondering if we should have sold the house in Kensington and left our Great Dane behind. Was that a sign that we wouldn't return to Georgetown until NIH grant renewed or disappeared altogether? Or was it possible to stay and work in Madrid? But working where, doing what? Francisco Franco was still in power in Spain, and we witnessed his gray uniformed guards ('los grises') beat up medical students to the ground without their knowing what the provocation was, as alleged. The research plans for an academic visitor on sabbatical leave were not clear. Helping technicians and personnel took siestas following their narcoleptic big lunches until 2:00 P.M. and then worked until 10:00 P.M. when their supper was light. Research was slow in Spain, but the basic science background of the medical students was far superior to their counterpart in the U.S. The opposite was true for the clinical training which was not as organized and effective as in continental U.S. ('Conus') America. Only the well 'connected' got the opportunity to make rounds and see patients with the clinical stars of the different departments.

We had three occasions to test this. First was when Angell Jr. developed a fulminant fever that required his tonsils to be removed stat! I couldn't believe we had to wait in line with other kids to have tonsils removed by an ENT specialist armed with an intraoral device to cut the tonsils out without any anesthesia other than ice cubes given them to taste while they waited in line. He nearly bled to death! Having that tonsil vessel branch cut so close to the carotid artery was a big risk to take. Poor kid! The next experience was almost as risky. I mentioned this before, but it is a memory I won't ever forget. My wife, Judy, was ready to deliver Barbara, our oldest daughter. She never had any serious complications when delivering the three boys, except Angell Jr. in New York. After a period of sedation with a mask connected to sodium pentothal, delivery was safe. At that time in Spain, women pushed, grunted, and yelled when delivering a baby. Judy was ready to take a plane back to the U.S.! Dr. Botella Llusia, the leading obstetrician at the time said, "Well, we have epidurals and we can provide the sedation but you have to set it up yourself. You ARE a doctor, aren't you?" I was petrified and sweated blood. I had a lab coat on, put some sterilized gloves on and a nurse helped me mix the IV drip and set it up to provide the sedation. Soon after that, there came that gorgeous madrileña I had also helped to deliver. Barbie was born! Last but by no means least, a crazy idea came into my mind. Since my research was not advancing very much, blaming the institutional siestas and all, maybe I could get the sabbatical leave to count as the equivalent of an internship and take the medical license exam. I had all the course work. Then I could practice medicine instead. The brainstorm did not last long. One Dr. Baena, an Asturian Internal Medicine professor from the University of Madrid Medical School agreed to let me follow him in his rounds, ask questions and participate in the discussions. I hated to deal with bleeding or infectious patients. I was reminded of my first undergraduate biology course when my professor insisted on my taking a live frog home in a shoe box so I could play with it during the weekend to get rid of my fear and pass the class. However, my theory exam grades were very good.

The real test came one day when after examining a cardiac patient with a stethoscope, we noticed the characteristic dry sound heard when liquid accumulates between two surfaces, the endocardium pressing hard on the contracting heart and the pericardium. The pericardial effusion had to be identified first before the fluid could be removed with a needle through the pericardium into the cavity avoiding perforating the endocardium into the heart cavity full of pressurized blood that would rush out upon contact with the needle. "Don't be afraid," Dr. Baena's high-pitched voice would repeat in a fatherly way, "You will notice that the plunger in the syringe will start coming up as it fills with clear pericardial fluid. Just wait. Then when the syringe fills up, it's easy." I thought to myself, scared to death, "Like hell it is." I took my lab coat off, never again to make rounds with Dr. Baena or anyone else, I swear. Everything became very frustrating, except watching Barbie grow in Madrid, before returning from the sabbatical back to my NIH grant at Georgetown Medical School in Washington, D.C.

While in Madrid, I never had the chance to meet and visit with Jimmy Ortiz, a West Point graduate and dear friend from high school who—at that time—was stationed at the U.S. Embassy in Madrid. But I had occasional contact with his friend in Puerto Rico, gynecologist Dr. Benjamin Curet, a buddy I had spent many hours listening to classical music with when growing up and who had connections with everybody. Being the son of a minister and member of a distinguished family of university professors, it was easy for him to recommend me for a faculty position at the medical school there. I had worked as an undergraduate assistant and lab instructor to his brother, Dr. Juan Daniel Curet, a Professor of Physical Chemistry at UPR before. Besides, the prospect of transferring my NIH grant to UPR made me more attractive as a candidate. If Georgetown U. opposed my leaving the position or demanded a reimbursement of sabbatical expenses, then I had to look again for a house near Georgetown, near the DC area. This uncertainty about a professional future would have been solved had I followed the prevalent materialistic approach and practiced a profession and got rich but, somehow, I felt my call was to investigate and assist in the formation of intelligent minds to lead future generations. Not that I detest the perks that come along with wealth, it was never my first priority. But I had to be practical and do whatever was necessary to sustain my beautiful family. My first academic priorities could perhaps wait until I retired when I would write for myself and share with anyone interested . . . . which I have done . . . . with no riches attached but with many controversial brainstorms, as the case may turn out to be, circulating around the HiQ communities for discussion and analysis.

CHAPTER 7

Once I became a regular faculty member at the state University of Puerto Rico Medical School, it made me feel odd. Here I find myself now as a professor at the same institution that put me on a waiting list when other more prestigious universities had accepted me without hesitation, but c'est la vie. Never look back, show your class, and labor hard. My uncle was smiling from Antares out there in the Scorpio constellation. Because of my biophysical background I was expected by Dr. Pinedo, head of Physiology and Biophysics Department and my boss, to join Dr. del Castillo at the Neurobiology Institute in Old San Juan where ionic fluxes across artificial membranes were being studied under voltage clamp conditions, among other things. My mathematics master's thesis on the kinetics of flow across body compartments would become handy.

As God would have it, my NIH grant at Georgetown University was not transferable to another institution and there was not enough money around to set up a lab for me. So, full-time research was out of the question. I had to spend time there with Dr. Pinedo's intestinal absorption studies and with Dr. del Castillo's membranes, when not lecturing or running the physiology labs. After work, I drove back from the then medical school building, next to the San Juan Capitol building, to the Valle Arriba Heights cul-de-sac in Carolina where my beautiful 5 bed-room house for four of us was facing a big park and made me relax, especially when the calm, relaxed demeanor of my wife took the stress out of me. Since our youngest daughter, Denise, was not born yet, everybody had their own private room. I felt proud that I was living in the town my Bobonis side of the family had founded years ago. My cousin, Papo, who owned an iron works shop, had transformed my spiral art design into protective iron doors covering the entire front of the house. Meanwhile the state university system was expanding and new campuses were opening across the island. The then president of the entire university system, Don Jaime Benitez, had somehow learned about my research frustrations, and my administrative abilities and unfulfilled dreams when I had set up the research lab at AFRRI's Department of Defense (DOD) facility and asked me if I would be interested in becoming a co-founder of a new university campus in Cayey, way up in the mountains of Cordillera Central where the old Henry Barracks military installation during the second world war was located. Judy was expecting our fifth child, Denise, and that would be an ideal place to raise a family. A colleague of mine at the medical school had singled me out as an ideal candidate to evaluate his new vasectomy procedure. It worked out, because Denise was my last child. To Cayey we went, along that sinuous mountain highway of so many memories, the 'Autopista'. Then, there, in the middle of that inter-mountainous valley, I was offered a strong brick house where the command officers used to live, all paid up, housing and utilities, as 'combat pay' for leaving the city and coming into that natural paradise where all of my five children grew up to become, in my fatherly-biased mind, the best citizens any nation can produce.

Thereafter, life was always a challenge. I had all the possible administrative positions academia could offer, from advisor to the university system president, to Chairman-Dean of Natural Sciences faculty, to Biology Department Head. However, I felt unable to effectively influence, in my typical non-political ways, the need to abandon that submissive colonial life style and choose liberty, either as a banana-like republic sans resources or a State of the American Union. No government would ever grant Puerto Rico the idealistic, tax free, Commonwealth status without having all states of the union claiming the same pipe dream status. Life in colonial, political Macondo, USA can be asphyxiating, the reason why, upon retirement, I had gone back into voluntary exile in Florida, USA. I had to. Now, this was the unique chance in a lifetime that would give -an idealist like me- the time to influence the formation of future generations of great men and women while marketing some of my crazy ideas on the brain dynamics of self-consciousness. At the same time, shaping and helping to improve the character features of young minds attracted me. This way, I would create consciousness of the importance of both public and private domains and how to avoid the excesses of both communism and monopolistic capitalism and their common greed for power and money at the expense of the involuntary needy. This also was a unique opportunity to provide the guidelines for searching for the pathways leading to the source(s) of righteousness by self-education. The monopolistic capitalism preached upon false principles. Greed had to be displayed as a clumsy exploitation apparatus pointed at a false goal, leaving the citizenry destitute of the proper just means/

criteria of comparative axiological principles and becoming prepared for a reasonable course in life where priorities are properly assigned by man's private powers through education. No doubt it should be invaluable in influencing the correct early formation of the individual character because it is in youth that we plant and later harvest our good and bad habits and prejudices and decide what trade or profession, pursuits, and matrimony suits our personal circumstances. What starts well ends well and if we are consistent, it will become the education of a wise man incapable of being turned into the cruel politician or professional warriors so damaging to the human race. The rules of prudence in ordinary affairs are learned first at home and developed while young. It is with the interaction with your fellow students that you learn not to be ashamed of your Taino, African, Arawak or European origin and you will be forever convinced of how unimportant all/any origin is to happiness, virtue, or greatness.

As Dean of the Faculty of Natural Sciences, I required that the most experienced professors include a course in basic sciences and spend time in shaping those young minds to be prepared for their eventual appearance upon a world stage. The means to achieve the proper goals then and later are as complex or simple as wisdom allows. Thus, we can choose either content and enjoyment as opposed to being stressed and tormented by regrets or regrettable impatience. We need to regulate our minds by practicing frugality, temperance and diligence. During my busy schedule investigating, lecturing and administrating, I found time to lecture on Neuropharmacology and Neurophysiology at the Ponce Medical School in southern Puerto Rico. I also wrote a monthly editorial column for the local newspapers in Spanish "El Mundo," and English "San Juan Star." I hope my own children understand why I had so little time to exchange tete-a-tete daily dialogues with them except on weekends when all seven of us occupied a whole pew on Sundays when attending Catholic mass in Montellano area of Cayey. It would be proper to say that the Cayey experience provided the multidisciplinary background so useful when attempting, upon retirement, to model a biopsychosocial frame into which existential reality could be better understood. Besides publishing two textbook volumes on Human Biology, I had managed also to publish at Editorial Limusa, Mexico, the basic elements on a biopsychosocial (BPS) model of consciousness that later on, upon retirement, would expand into 4 volumes on the "Neurophilosophy of Consciousness." I spent every free minute inside my office at the mountain university, looking at Cuco, the bull statue that decorated the entrance to the old Natural Sciences building, and reading library books which afforded me the means of improvement by constant study. I also set at least a couple of hours each day for peaceful, isolated meditation. The geographical isolation of that beautiful valley in the mountains, Cayey provided the kind of setting conducive to a reclusive life that kept me away from taverns, games, and frolics of any kind. My commitment to have the best undergraduate Natural Sciences faculty in the whole UPR system continued indefatigable, besides my higher commitment to a young family of five gorgeous, healthy children growing up to be educated in the future.

Judy was a very studious person herself and would never complain about things most people would, a stoic attitude that worried me. But, it was indeed lucky for me that I could count on her as another one much disposed to intellectual growth and frugality as I. A cell biologist herself, who later successfully completed a law degree in Spanish, not her native tongue, was commendable. We studied together and became lawyers at the same time. She assisted me cheerfully in the discussion and evaluation of many a brainstorm regarding my limited research activities with students or curriculum design. Her constant reading of philosophy, her minor *concentration at St. Claire College in Minnesota, was seen by our children as a bold and arduous project of arriving at moral and ethical perfection. I, personally, had to depend on my natural inclination, upbringing, custom or enterprise activity and how it might influence or lead me into rightful decisions.

As a faculty dean, the undertaking was at times more difficult than I had imagined. Dealing with prima-donna professors coming from the United States, North, Central and South America—and many from Spain-, made me realize I had to be very careful because of cultural sensibilities. To be completely virtuous was not sufficient enough to prevent our occasional misunderstandings. This meant biting your tongue, avoiding controversial military habits that had to be broken and substituted for good interactive civilian ones also acquired and established. With my wife's constant help, I was able to gradually depend on a steady, uniform rectitude of professional academic conduct. That never stopped me from always behaving like that shy, reclusive and idealistic loner many a times taken to be a snooty, conceited knight riding on his high horse. But I never abused my high positions. It was tempting at times to remind the science specialists, especially mathematic experts, that they also had to be cultured into other humanistic areas so important in the transformation of young students into well-informed and effective future leaders. I designed an 'integrated science' curriculum where all professors were invited to participate and were required to root their contributions of science content in their historical evolution to the present time. Many colleagues hated the idea of having to update their knowledge on how things were, how they were presently, and how they were likely to become. In the process, knowing they were dealing with college freshmen, they had to hone their essential virtues and, not only master the content, but face the challenge of a clear transmission to un-experienced young minds. This required a good dosage of fortitude, industry, sincerity, moderation, justice temperance, order, chastity and humility. In my personal case, after five children, I had to concentrate on industry and frugality precedence because of outstanding debts, and the need for saving for rainy days. I had been thoroughly trained at and exposed to the rest of the virtues at my uncle's house. Needless to say, with the advantage of hindsight, I never arrived at the perfection I had been so ambitious in obtaining for others, and in fact, a few trivial bad habits hardened and became incorrigible. But the fact that I tried, by living an exemplary life with all of my family, influenced others, and it was later recognized with university plaques after my retirement. All of my children grew healthy and happy inside that Cayey faculty 'country club' as many envious local residents chided. Security gates, 24/7 guard protection, swimming pool, free house and utilities and a beautiful landscape, and of course Judy, was a gift from God.

Angell Jr., the tall, oldest child, was finishing high school across the street. His entrance exam for the state university was "number one" for the region. His same high record was obtained for the Asvab Navy aptitude test. Little did I know that, upon graduation, he had it all figured out to accept special electronics training by the Naval school in Chicago. I drove him to the airport soaking my shirt with tears. We were a close-knit family.

When time came for the rest of our children to go to college, we moved back to Carolina, but this time to a three-story, fully-equipped and furnished building with an outside office, where we lived, worked and also rented. There was a beautiful office on the first floor from where my wife and I practiced law. I would handle the medical malpractice cases part time because I travelled daily on the highway to reach the university campus in Cayey while our kids went to college. Johnny was attending Hotel Administration School, Daniel went to Architecture School, Barbie specialized in Plastic Arts at UPR, and Denise earned first prize Valedictorian in high school and then registered as an honor student at UPR, following in my steps. Meanwhile, I was exhausted travelling many miles back and forth along highway 52 to Cayey, lecturing at

Ponce Medical School, writing articles for two newspapers, writing a book, and preparing and litigating cases.

Like her older brother Angell Jr., Denise developed 'wanderlust' and went to the University of North Carolina in Greenville, North Carolina as an exchange student. She earned her Bachelor's degree in Kinesiology there as a regular student. That left Daniel, Johnny, and Barbie in our household to care for while they finished their university degrees at the University of Puerto Rico main Campus. What Judy and I considered an Hispanic-Irish extended family tradition, was later on, upon returning back to the continental U.S., considered as an over-protective strategy that would interfere with the ingrained North American tradition of self-sufficiency 'out of the nest'.

Meanwhile Angell Jr. continued travelling all over *the world aboard a US Aircraft carrier, and Denise completed her studies and eventually had a short-lived marriage to a local, wealthy North Carolinian. As the political situation in colonial Macondo, USA turned intolerable, and still is, we couldn't wait to return back to the continental U.S. We built a lake-front home in Deltona, Florida where I still live. I was not ready for retirement and couldn't find an equivalent university position in Florida, so my family went ahead of me, and I became a commuting professor between Deltona, Florida and Cayey, Puerto Rico. I couldn't wait to return to my family and stay there. I missed them terribly. I counted the days until retirement every day but maintained an expensive transatlantic telephone conversation with wife as often as possible.

The only one to be affected by the move to Deltona was Johnny, who was only able to finish half of the 4-year Bachelors Degree curriculum in Hotel Administration sponsored by Cornell University at UPR. He would have preferred the Hispanic way of life. This was in sharp contrast to the time when, having moved to Puerto Rico from the U.S., he did not understand a word in Spanish. While taking classes at a catholic academy under Ms. Santa-Pinter, an Argentinian teacher, who wrongly thought he had some learning problems, he was forced to sit in front of the classroom on a high chair for everyone to laugh at. This was a cruel experience that affected him to the very end of his shortened life. Before designing our beautiful lake-front house in Deltona, Florida, Daniel was doing architectural design work for Zalloumco Construction, a custom-made design challenge where he developed his fine architectural skills. He and Angell Jr. were the first ones to move into our house after Angell Jr. had accumulated overdoses of Ibuprofen which ruined his renal function. At that time, the cold war was raging, and after leaving the navy, he was gainfully employed by a Washington, D.C. based Martin and Marietta Company in support of the cold war effort. When the cold war froze, he lost his job and his incapacitating health problems began. The unprecedented Middle Eastern problems and global awakening were brewing, and the quality of life began to decline. It turned out to be so for almost everyone else in sunny Florida, where all white elephants traditionally come to die.

CHAPTER

I had no idea what was waiting for all of us in sunny Florida upon retirement. I was lost without a secretary, a lab assistant and without any experience or ability for cooking, mowing the lawn or keeping a house account. Judy had spoiled all of us and now she was not feeling well. This frustration was picked up in my first medico-legal novel in the English language, "The Duplex House." There I describe the early stages of a transition from a busy productive professional life to a busy but non-productive home life. After being interviewed and offered a job as a Social Security judge in Orlando, Florida, I was ignored when they found out I was a card carrying registered Republican voter. I then found a job lecturing Anatomy and Physiology at a University of Central Florida (UCF) campus, and now Daytona State College, to keep up with the rapidly evolving field that applied to the brain. Also, the rapidly developing computer technology satiated my appetite for knowledge anew. There were many family health problems to solve, but I was not intimidated by the seeming magnitude of the undertaking ahead of me. Fortitude and forbearance always work great changes and accomplish great results if one first develops contingency plans. Amid all these evolving health problems, I had plans of going back to my first vocations as an undergraduate—philosophy and music. I would again become an industrious and frugal recluse and, by cutting off all dolce-vita amusements and other employments that would distract and divert my attention away from the execution of that dream, I had promised myself to develop as a life plan a theory of self-consciousness. My original plan to continue the piano training I had started early on with famed pianist Carmelina Figueroa at the free music schools (Escuelas Libres de Musica) failed. It failed because, while the theory was relatively easy, performing now and then felt like I was using 10 cramped thumbs. So I continued the collection of symphonic masterpieces I had started at age nine when one song would fit into one side of the hard plastic disk and later on a symphony fit into both sides of a long-playing record. Now we have many choices at Internet music radio. As Angell Jr. continued living with renal-failure complications, it was very hard for me to watch my oldest son suffer, and I donated one of my kidneys to him, a drama described in "The Duplex House" novel. Judy had recovered from her breast cancer removal and chemotherapy and was enjoying life in our beautiful 7 bedroom house by Lake Louise where I still live. I pondered about what better thing I could do than follow the path my destiny had traced for my mission. This mission my uncle had expected me to follow, whatever that was, in which he trusted I would excel and make my contribution to posterity . . . . if possible. But first, I had to get acquainted with Deltona and some of its then few hundred inhabitants. India Boulevard was empty, and our house was built after they put a post light in front of the only other existing house along the boulevard, across the street.

Deltona was an unincorporated piece of land, a bedroom community for Orlando, where everything happened in Central Florida. So, before I dug in I began now to turn my thoughts to community affairs, beginning with health, utilities, public safety, and available jobs for my adult children. I joined the community council that preceded the now controversial City Council initiated a couple of years later when Deltona became an incorporated territory under the leadership of John Masiarschik. Deltona today is the largest city in Volusia County with almost 90 thousand inhabitants, no major industry, and full of spoiled youngens and politicians-for-sale. On the whole, we were satisfied with being established here in the boondocks even though we regretted there being at that time no provision for a hospital, college for a complete education of youth, no civic organizations nor supermarkets. There was a church on practically every other major street and a good library. The Deltona Inn, near the exit from I-4 corridor, was the only place of entertainment. West of Deltona, across the I-4 corridor, was Orange City and beautiful Debary which followed the contours of the St. John's River on its sinuous and meandering path to the north into the Atlantic Ocean at Jacksonville. Before its trip north St. John's River separated Volusia County from Seminole County's Sanford Marina to the south and Lake County on the west side. To get to know the community I renewed my membership with American Mensa, rejoined the Knights of Columbus near our parish, Lady of the Lakes, the Rotary Club and the Elks. These same organizations had provided in Puerto Rico a safe social outlet for our family to socialize and we hoped for the same outcome here in Deltona. We were active at the Community Council and it didn't take long for Florida Fish Memorial Hospital to set foot nearby at Orange City and the Daytona

Beach Community College (now Daytona State College) to flourish as the city didn't stop growing. Daniel was establishing a good name designing expensive houses for the growing areas surrounding Deltona. Angell Jr. was in a stable condition working as distributor for a major company and Johnny worked as an apprentice assistant manager with a pizza company while Barbie designed flower displays for a Loews store. I then embarked on a follow-up on my previous publication with Limusa Editorial, Biopsicosociologia. However, I was lost trying to adapt to life in Central Florida, a long shot from what our family had experienced in NYC, Spain, Bethesda, MD or Puerto Rico. There was something different in the sociology of Deltona that merits mentioning and explains our surprise at seeing so many churches when we first came here. All kinds of different church denominations, including the catholic church in different locations, were busily involved in community building, from assemblies in the open air subject to bad weather forecasts to meetings inside closed old buildings where persons were appointed to receive contributions destined to procure the ground and erect the definitive building, where the congregation was to meet in prayer and important community work. Isolated communities always have unemployed labor, broken shop-keepers and several other insolvent debtors, including several illegal immigrants of indolent and idle habits, or paroled out of crowded jails. If you were not in the health or fast food industry, there was little to do except clearing land, cutting cane, or peddling illegal drugs. Deltona was pretty clean in that respect. Preachers of the Baptist faith were pretty good in running their charities and always made large collections. Their down-to-earth, grass roots eloquence had a wonderful mesmerizing power over the hearts and purses of the congregation, wherever assembled.

Judy, after a double mastectomy from cancer just before my retirement, began showing signs of a relapse that would finally take her away and precipitate my tragic emotional downfall as described in my second medico-legal novel written in English, "The 15th Sunday of Extraordinary Time." From then on, I felt just like I did when my Uncle Agustin died. The floor had fallen from under my feet and I was freely falling or floating in space. After almost half a century with the same good woman, one can never forget. As Judy's health progressively declined, all my children began drinking more often, and this may have contributed to Johnny's ongoing hepatic ailment that confined him to an involuntary sedentary life of disability and eventual untimely death. When I got really involved with my wife's recurrence of cancer and my growing investigation of brain dynamics, I had to disengage myself from city and county affairs, especially after I had tried to run for the City Council of my district and withdrew once I knew someone else was also running for same District 5. Besides, I felt I had earned and secured some leisure time during the rest of my life for philosophical studies and family amusements. I purchased a fully equipped computer with all peripherals and software perks, and proceeded in my "thoughts experiments" with great alacrity. But, as is natural, my family and close friends now often laid hold of me for their medico-legal problems, at times imposing some duty upon me to investigate or draft a document which I dutifully complied with.

CHAPTER

9

At the time my dear wife, Judy, was not improving after her breast cancer had returned with a vengeance, I was also getting ready for donating a kidney to my older son. My youngest daughter was having marital problems and my oldest daughter left our house in Deltona to join her in Greenville, North Carolina. I had to get my mind busy to avoid being mentally crushed by my own emotional feelings like I feel now after the untimely death of my two oldest sons. Deep concentration isolates you temporarily from your existential problems. Besides, I had been for some time now preparing myself to synthesize my ideas on reality and consciousness upon retirement. I thought I could pick up inherited genetic DNA memory, perceptual sensory input, acquired memetic memory, conceptual inferential input (based on language processing), and the associated emotional mind state all into one comprehensive hybrid biopsychosocial (BPS) physical/metaphysical package embracing the physical ontological and the metaphysical epistemological, and weaving it together by the quasi deterministic glue of quantum theory that left room for free will and a credible explanation for self-consciousness. A big project indeed! I would avoid mentioning my Catholic religion because I was convinced it was not necessary, and I could use the same arguments nonbelievers use to prove my point and be more convincing thereby. I was determined to prove that a belief in God was subject to rational logic analysis as a strategy for biopsychosocial (BPS) survival as a species. Somehow, we had to escape the classical dogma that only the human mind sensations and rationality constituted the exclusive cognitive faculty. I had to find what was in between, how the sense-phenomenal "perceptual" input was coded into general neuronal network representations expressing the universality of the otherwise direct, singular objects/events immediately presented to our senses in the environmental niche and how their corresponding "conceptual" inferences also find their way into general neuronal network representations expressing the indirect, mediate, attributions and explanations about their meaning to the body economy in the biological, psychic and social (BPS) spectrum. The search for meaning was to be found with the aid of language sentential or symbolic logic representations making possible the co-generation of self-consciousness and the associated mental state corresponding to the judgment in relation to the sense-phenomenal (internal or external) input, genetic/memetic memory input, and their associated emotional mental state. Ideally, each input would be dynamically and globally integrated and the resulting package would be dynamically updated and be retrieved from cortical attractor spaces on short notice as our adaptive judgment on a given contingency. Sensibility to the body proper "internal" and the environmental "external," as a bottoms-up process would now include not only sense-phenomenal intero, extero and propioreceptors inputs, but also transfinite inputs into quantum electromagnetic energy absorbers like DNA or RNA! I felt like I was spreading myself too thin until I would asymptotically get to know everything about nothing! The heads-down process of understanding the meaning entailed the emergence of self-consciousness with the help of the silent inner proto language generated in the language processing. I was convinced that what has escaped the imagination of most of my colleagues has been the realization that both the perceptual input, bottoms-up and the conceptual, heads-down processes are severely limited in their content and capacity for resolution in our human species. Thus, when making judgments about optimal adaptive spatiotemporal responses to important contingencies, we can no longer have certainty about the truth value of our input or output content or meaning respectively, we only have probabilities. We have no choice but to satisfy that human innate curiosity about our origins and destiny and make mental representations of that micro sub-Planckian and macro cosmological invisibilities with the aid of metaphysical epistemological logic tools and cross our fingers. Ergo, the ontology value of an un-aided scientific methodology is complemented / supplemented by epistemology because understanding and sensibility are both sub-served by the faculty of modeling with a hybrid epistemontological approach which I had promised myself to develop. Thus, incomplete in the absolute sense as they are, the practical reason that Kant defended must be now reinterpreted to include evolving explanations on the structure/function of the invisible, non-existential reality that includes theological and physicalist faiths. The cognitive processing undertaken by the rational faculty depends on the quality of the bottoms-up information to produce the logical inferences underlying our head-down modal judgments, hopefully consistent and coherent, within the context of our biopsychosocial existential reality. And this is necessarily reflected in our evolving legal codes and constitutions. It is clear that the self-conscious affirmation of one's existence, the "I" actor and observer, is situated at the executive vortex where all relevant perceptual/conceptual representations converge as the synthesis of the several semantic constituents of that cognition into the high order cognitive singularity content in a cortical premotor attractor space ready to be consciously chosen to activate the corresponding muscles or glands into executive adaptive action. How these primitive representations in the form of a-priori logical constructs are assembled within the existential circumstance and ongoing mental state of the subject and made available for free will access and choice may be outside the reach of rational tools, and I anticipate much trouble examining what I consider the most crucial human cognitive faculty. The most difficulty will no doubt be to explain the induction of the self-conscious state with the language faculty and assigning a cooperative role to synaptic and electromagnetic quantum processing. It's a brave new world we are all witnessing. The comfort of the quotidian existence under the Boolean world of truth or falsity and certainty has evolved into the stressful uncertainty of a statistical probabilistic world where disjunctive and conditional statements always enter the decision-making process to preserve the truth-functional structure of logical reasoning. Many of us, whose hobby is to model reality, have to always keep in focus that our most serious brainstorm pronouncements are necessarily inferences on representations and never descriptions of observable falsifiable reality. In the bottoms-up phase, our brains represent inner and outer objects and events inputs for linguistic processing into other types of metaphysical logic representations and the heads-down output are only inferences, only representing a mediate cognition of that original object/event. Our judgment on a given situation, i.e., our opinion, is thereby the result of representations of previous representations until one final concept binds many representations and worse, many concepts may comprehend a single representation. Our judgments are far from being objective. They are inferential and subjective. That is the best our species can offer in the matter of cognitive certainty. That fact of life when combined with another fact of life, our innate curiosity about our species origin and destination, necessarily makes room for beliefs and faiths, theological, physicalist or whatever. I had much difficulty marketing this unpopular idea among nontheists. Not less difficult was my attempt at developing a convincing formulation where I had to settle for the simultaneous cogeneration link between proto language (inner language) processing and self-consciousness as just a convenient explanation for the invisible processes outside my limits of corroboration as to the details. Marketing these concepts to multidisciplinary audiences is most difficult, especially when dealing with theoretical physicists and mathematicians who would not accept that their physicalist constructs are in themselves 'beliefs' not radically different from classical symbolic or sentential logic representations leading to belief-type 'propositions'. These latter types can be as fallible and uncertain as the former and, considering their intended influence on social conviviality, both may be considered as subjectively necessary and sufficiently unfeasible propositions. Ultimately, they are both the result of unconscious genetic, subconscious memetic processing of bottoms-up inputs (from internal and external objects or events) into neuronal network representations, including their assignment of agreed-upon language-related label descriptions or attributions predicated on their size, shape, color, etc. to be followed by conceptual elaborations predicated on those or related previous representations of same objects/events in memory. At this level, the functional copula subject-predicate (object/event description or action, e.g., table is red, chair is moving) allows for the formation of logical language rules according to which judgments are expressed in a logical syntax and semantic form necessary for communication in a given language. Ergo, both propositions and beliefs are ultimately inferences about an invisible world derived from the use and application of pure laws of logic and expressed in a predication copular format (subject-predicate, modal-conditional). Coetaneous with the modifications leading to the final structuring according to truth-functional value considerations, a self-conscious identification with such circumstantial consideration ensues. In this respect, I took issue with Chomsky's syntax-semantic vector in formulating sentential logic. They defended the vector based on the primacy of the innate primitive biological self-preservation imperative 'meanings' ('intension') controlling syntax considerations. They neglect the influence which depend on the idiosyncrasies of the adopted language structure. Curiously, the actors behind the recent advances in technology have given low priority to issues only capable of being expressed in modal or conditional logic formats, especially when the brain's emotional states, resisting logical formulations, exert a causal influence on the outcome of a decision to act or not. Somehow physical theoreticians seem to conveniently ignore the inexorable presence of real-life existentialist component (emotions) in every significant human judgment. Unfortunately, it is not so much about the legitimacy of a rational, truth-valued, unified composite of objective, meaningful and relevant parts defining a claim about the ideal world as much as it is about how the lonely leader and his emotional mental state circumstance will translate into the needs of the society he represents vis-a-vis his own. The logically structured, semantically well arranged, truth-valued judgment representing the best legal and moral, biological, psychic and social interests of a collective is only a goal in clear controversy with the biopsychosocial needs of the individualized components of the collective. All propositional 'facts' or theological 'beliefs' are of necessity inferences about the visible and invisible aspects of existential reality, life inside an epistemontological hybrid reality we cannot escape from. Ergo, existential reality does not exclusively equate with objective reality. The former is an acceptable, subjective constraint of reality in se whose absolute truth and meaningful values are only apparent. On the other hand, how accurate and 'objective' can the human brain representations of objects/events be? Especially when further constrained by the imposed linguistic compositionality in which it must be expressed in both inner and reported modes using the subject's proto-rational syntax/semantic straight jacket. Thus, claimed 'objective judgments' thus elaborated are not to be confused with the symbolic or sentential logic "truth" of their representations as materialist physicalists would have us believe. Logical consistency is a necessary but insufficient part of the totality. Symbolic or sentential logic representations of the invisibility of the noumenal or cosmological reality can be rationally intelligible yet truly valueless. "Truth" is a goal to be achieved as we travel the sinuous path along an evanescent asymptotic line. Consequently, we can only have opinions on the probable value of our representations of an invisible reality, and that is as close as we can go about knowing the truth of our absolute reality. We can only aim at an isomorphic correspondence between the structure / function of an object/event and the symbolic/sentential logic representation as expressed in a syntax/semantic copula we call an 'intensional' explanation or opinion, not a description which we reserve for sense-phenomenal entities. This means that the brain cannot produce absolute truths whether analytical (in differentiating), synthetic (in integrating) representations before the facts (a-priori) or after the empirical facts (a-posteriori). For all men and rabbits all empirically based, synthetic judgments (a posteriori) are the result of subconscious processing and can, in theory, be programmed in a computer. They relate more to the guarantee of biological survival of the species as they interact with a potentially hostile phenomenological environment with limited necessary resources. At the exclusively human level where psychosocial considerations become part of the survival equation we have to resort to, brain representations of the chaos of sensations, and access an innate language faculty to classify, sort, combine, permute and parse to extract the meaning of an otherwise atemporal, acausal and asymmetric reality 'in se'. Genetic and memetic memories of past and present provide the bottoms-up input of coded representations to evolve probable alternatives of adaptive responses to future contingencies to be freely chosen by consent from preexistent dynamic probabilities in a cortical attractor space reservoir. In the process both language and self-consciousness are cogenerated. The participation of the amygdala, hippocampus, thalamus and limbic system in the formulation and synthesis of the representations (in harmony with natural law) into neocortical phase spaces has to be detailed and remains as a great challenge to cage into a credible formulation. The materialist physicalist need not be challenged by a hybrid, epistemontological model of reality because, as Kant admonished, conceptual thoughts without perceptual meaningful content (intensions) are empty just like a pure physical ontology without a metaphysical epistemology is blind. The indelible complementary/supplementary and semantic interactivity of perceptual and conceptual (ontology, epistemology) is of the essence for an existential cognitive act to take place, for neither senses can conceptualize nor rationality sense. However, all human species limitations in perceptual / conceptual resolution being considered, it is fair to say that there may be conceptual meanings without rational underpinnings (intuitions) or perceptual experiences that resist their formal expression as logical constructs (revelations?). Should they be considered empty, bogus or meaningless and denied cognitive status? Just like quantum theory—nowadays the best 'scientific methodology'—cannot qualify as being exclusively and objectively valid, it is nonetheless rationally intelligible about the invisibility of a sub-Planckian reality containing massless 'objects'! Unlike this case, theological theist experiences cannot be combined with ontological measurements to generate quasi objective valid arguments as is the case also with brain dynamic modeling. But recorded history and human experience of negentropy has validated the anthropo-centered, self-referential non-conceptual intuitions we know as religious beliefs. The Cartesian type of truth preferred by materialists would leave no room for scientific or religious beliefs in that it requires the actual sense-phenomenal verification of the object/event being precisely reduced to symbolic/ sentential representations in its physical absence. Beliefs, by and large, are defeasible and subject to evolutionary modifications. Moderation requires that beliefs be subjectively and objectively sufficient and coherent with sets of other beliefs. In theory propositions may be false yet the believer—theoretical physicist or mystic—can demonstrate that his conviction is operationally justified until revoked in the lab or in the social ecosystem niche. The embodied finitude of the human species condition justifies more cognitive flexibility. And this includes a consideration of the inseparability of the human emotional affect at all stages during the elaboration of a final judgment, a very difficult element to include/formulate into the equation. The judging capacities of the existential human being in his circumstantial milieu cannot be ignored by self-serving purists. I hope this emphasis on human existential realities is not construed as a free willing Sartrian type of existentialism. It simply means that the logical format of Fodorian 'propositional attitudes' formulations has to emphasize more on sense-phenomenal content at the expense of self-serving logical format. But, for the purpose of communication we need to categorize ongoing sense-phenomenal perceptions within the framework of an agreed-upon universal a priori referential for the purpose of providing guiding rules for the evaluation of objective truth content, freed—when possible—from irrelevant modal or affective 'non sequiturs', reminiscent of the Kantian 'Categorical Imperatives' controlling the participation of fallacies and moral sins in the formulation of propositions. It may be necessary to psychologize modality in the structure of the subject-predicate copula if it helps identifying the semantic content of a judgment. It is difficult to distinguish propositional attitudes from logic modality. A predicate monadic logic concentrating on 'intensional' content is sufficient for our limited purposes of a brain quantum dynamics model. It is important to realize that, because human existential reality is in the brain, an understanding of its dynamics must start with the raw data of sense-phenomenal impressions, in the style of empiricist philosophy. But these sensory impressions are limited in conveying information about the structure/function of existential reality. So, to compensate for ontological deficiencies in resolution we need to complement/supplement the paucity of facts with an epistemological rationalist approach based on credible meta sensorial, probable but defeasible / revocable facts as found in metaphysical logic propositional representations, as stated above. After all, not all cognitions arise from sensory data but also from innate genetic memory, acquired memetic memories or a combination thereof. The epistemological component of the 'hybrid' approach I am suggesting will accommodate whatever logical procedure there is available that brings you the closest to an original sense-phenomenal description. This may take the cognitive format of substituting the invisible 'form' for its visible 'effects'. This transition from a sensory 'description' (what) to an inferred 'explanation' (how) as an acceptable identification has two modes in their order of reliability: logical and natural supervenience between the invisible object/ event X and the credible manifestation of its inferred presence by logical induction or a measurable and falsifiable effect Y. How does an invisible X relates/determines Y? Ideally one can isolate X logically but not in nature. X will have a strict causal determination of Y iff X features are necessary and sufficient to generate Y features such that changes (form or semantic content) in Y will cause a corresponding change in X. In brain dynamic studies we have only a limited number of ways of establishing the relationship between the X variable of interest (e.g., anger, interest, inhibition/activation, etc.) and Y a measured (increased circulation, metabolism, electrical activity, etc.) or behavioral effect (crying, laughing, etc.) as a function of a controlled input (sensory/ environmental or spoken/semantic) by the investigator. When these a-posteriori cognitive responses are elicited in the absence of sensory impressions we suspect they respond to innate or an unidentified a-priori input. So long as mathematics is a valuable language tool to represent objects/events in their absence or 'represent' other representations, semantic judgments, a-priori or not, depend on their original tangible content and not on the language tool. It should also be noticed that sensory modalities are neutral and only the circumstantial reality of the actor makes them meaningful or not, as registered in the output/behavior.

CHAPTER

10

It took some time for me to finally realize that retirement was an entirely different ball of wax when making household decisions. I had to adopt an entirely different mindset to see and effectively interact with wife, children, pets and their old and current controversies 24/7. Now there were no secretaries, assistants, student helpers, etc. to help me run my ship and enjoy the pleasures of a leisurely plan-ahead for the content of new courses, labs, curricula and other perks. This was a new world I was not prepared to adapt to, least to lead. This feeling was reflected in my afore-mentioned medico-legal novel venture in the English language, "The Duplex House." To make things worse, at that time, my wife was getting worse from the cancer chemotherapy onslaught and my older son was ready for a kidney transplant. How can any retired human being suffer like this and still be able to sink into the deepest levels of conceptual abstraction? This was reflected in my Volume I of "Neurophilosophy of Consciousness" book where I essentially outlined the various possible routes towards understanding the problem I was about to tackle and never really resolved. You can practice wingless flying over the fence or your neighbor's house, but you will never take off from your lawn except in the virtual reality of your dreams. Soon after I donated a kidney to my son and lived through a near death experience after an intoxication with an overdose of an opiate, life became a Via Crucis watching my saintly wife slowly dying. Even the heavens protested when four hurricanes visited us in Florida soon after she finally died at the lakefront house where she wanted to be for this moment of transfiguration, our hands firmly held together until hers lost their grip and I held my breath. Judy had passed away . . . That Christmas, I spent seven sleepless days and nights fasting with peanuts and red Pinot Noir and writing, non-stop, my mea culpa novel "The 15th Sunday of Extraordinary Time." I dedicated it to that great Irish lady who gave her life to raise my five children and bring out the best of my feelings and creative potential. Soon thereafter, all my pets died also, and I wished I could have joined her in that special abode she must have in the highest of virtual heavens. We all still miss her and know she is looking down, watching over our three remaining children and her idealistic Quixotic husband that was. The more depressed I felt, the more I needed to get involved in abstract theoretical insights that would mesmerize and capture all my attention. I also underwent psychological treatment during my bereavement at the local Hospice facilities.

CHAPTER

After being married to my first wife for forty-five + years, I was devastated when she died in July 2004. I joined a Hospice Support Group that met on Saturday mornings. There were nine of us who met and shared our grief for an hour each week. One hot summer Saturday in August, 2006, we met a new member of our group, Suzi Beauchamp, who had lost both her son and husband in January of same year. She walked in wearing a white sun dress that I will never forget. Even though she was also grieving, she had a great sense of humor and complained about the terrible coffee in a joking way that brought laughter to our group. After hearing her tell of the two deaths she had recently endured, I decided immediately that I was drawn to her and wanted to take her under my wing to help her. The following Thursday, I called her and asked if she would like to go with me for a sandwich at the Florida, Deland Elks. She hesitated and stated she wasn't ready to begin dating but I said, "I'm not asking you for a date—just a sandwich. You have to eat you know." She finally agreed and that began our complex but happy lives together. We were married the following October 2007 at my house with our support group and intimate friends and family in attendance. When Suzi became my second wife, an entirely different but necessary chapter in my secluded but safe cage opened in my life. I would come out of my sheltered cocoon and face real, unsheltered life. Meanwhile I had already finished and published the Volume II of the series "Neurophilosophy of Consciousness, An Epistemontological View of Reality." Could I abandon my search or continue my obsession with trying to make a path as I walked? Would my new wife accept my isolation and my bigamous life with my computer-wife? I tried to answer some questions on quantum-based brain dynamics, and in the process, there came more questions to answer than I had bargained for when I started. Would Suzi, that outgoing, beautiful fashion model from North Carolina and Virginia, ever understand the silently grieving, shy, conservative loner? A carefully groomed and fed veritable household zoo of dogs, cats, birds, ducks, egrets and other lake-front mammals, and every flower, bush and tree growing inside and outside the large house would keep her distracted from me and her own family issues . . . . most of the time. Meanwhile, I continued my grope brain dynamics studies in between emergency health problems with my two ailing sons, Johnny and Angell, Jr., who were then living in Daniel's house on Sullivan Street in Deltona, Florida. Daniel had been deployed to Iraq, another constant worry for all of us even though this time he was a specialty consultant for the Department of defense with no other weapon than a folded newspaper when walking inside a terrorist infiltrated compound! Difficult times indeed. Suzi was the opposite of my first wife, Judy. She was an extrovert, always finding something to talk about, outgoing with our friends, and unable to sit still and relax. Judy was quiet, a homebody who was afraid of having company in our home. She loved to read and was content to be with her family. Suzi brought friends over for dinners, loved to go dancing, sang karaoke, and loved people. She brought two cats with her but added two more plus a dog. At first I was. exhausted trying to keep up with her, but I finally realized that she had opened- up a new world vision to me that I had not known before, and 1 began to enjoy and learn new things in our new life together. Since Judy had been sick for several years before her death, our house was in much need of some TLC. This was Suzi's priority. She began painting the rooms and redecorating everything in sight. She had brought her own furnishings from her house when she moved into my house and began blending hers with mine, a feat I had no clue would work. But it did. Then she started on the yard and landscape, sometimes working into the darkness to finish a project. She and her son, Don, wall-papered the bathroom and she bought new mirrors and fixtures for that. I was amazed at how nice everything looked. I teased her about making our home into a "museum." Suzi had several collections—bisque doves, Pillsbury dough boys, tea pots, dinner bells and many figurines and "dust collectors." However, she managed to incorporate them into her decorating scheme that appeared uncluttered and tasteful. As l worked on my computer, I watched her in action and was exhausted just observing her energy and expertise, now somewhat diminishing as aging and morbidities encroached upon her. At one time in her life, Suzi had been a fashion model and had also owned her own florist shop. She had also had some rough times during her early years that she often talked about. She had raised three sons and prior to moving to Florida, had attended nursing school and worked in the hospital in Fredericksburg, Virginia, and had worked in a couple of doctors' offices. In addition, she had done home health care and been a caregiver to her mother and ailing husband all at the same time. She also worked in a florist twice a week just to "play in the flowers" and enjoy the respite from all the family sicknesses. When she moved to Florida, she began teaching school part time as a respite while she was caregiver to her husband who was dying of prostate cancer. Her husband died January 11, 2006 in Florida, two weeks after she buried one of her sons in Virginia. In December 2007, Suzi's mother, now in her 90's, was suffering from very poor health in North Carolina. We brought her to live with us against her mother's wishes and Suzi made her last months of life bearable and fun until her death in April, 2008. I was then able to see another side of Suzi, her caring and loving soft side that had not been so obvious to me before. This same Suzi became my rock when my two sons became so ill prior to their untimely deaths in 2012. She mothered all of them. She continues to "mother" all of our pets, from the indoor pets to her "outdoor" ducks, cranes and birds. When one of her mother ducks was killed by a car, Suzi helped another mother duck raise 37 ducklings in 2009. Pet food controlled our marital budget as it became as expensive as our own food. IRS would not accept pets as dependents . . . At this writing, we are both still grieving our losses and occasionally escape out to dance and enjoy our friends. Suzi has slowed down a little and has discovered that being retired means doing some of the things she always wanted to do but never had time for. We have traveled a little, something we both enjoy, and settled into a life of more leisure. I realize that I have been greatly blessed by the two wives in my life, each one opposite from the other in character but similar in the things that really count in Christian living. It was time to continue with my neurophilosophy investigations.

I had previously been warned about the technological explosion of the post computer, late 20th century age, and the cognitive strangle-hold theoretical particle physicists had on controlling science/natural philosophy evolution into the 21st century. I always liked to stand on solid firm ground before my mind soars into the virtual domain of open-ended abstractions. In real life, a good car mechanic may be more important than the physics professor. specialized in auto mechanics when it comes to fixing my damaged real car. In the study of consciousness we have many problems to solve in the physiology of the brain even before we understand how it works as a causal mind executive. But theorizing about how the mind processes sensory input and executes an adaptive solution transcends the immediate and sets the strategy for solving ALL putative and related problems that may arise. But you still require hands-on knowledge about the structure/function of the car/brain the way a mechanic/professional does. When, upon retirement you work alone and when this search is translated into mind/ body relationships neither the bright logic mathematician nor the skilled neurosurgeon alone will perform in a satisfactory way unless you go multidisciplinary and constantly fear spreading yourself too thin. But it was better than knowing everything about the computer formulations applicable to brain dynamics by studying more and more about less and less until asymptotically you knew everything about nothing! Anyway, it was going to be hard multidisciplinary work, but I needed the challenge to escape my emotional pain and chose the super complex hybrid epistemontological way. This decision required choosing the logical foundations of my 'existential' approach. My conclusions would hopefully be falsifiable in the laboratory measurements and/or verifiable on the metaphysical logic desk. Ideally my judgments on self-consciousness would be of the synthetic a-posteriori variety leaving to mathematicians the analytic a—priori computer processing of their symbolic/sentential logic representations which did not require their familiarity with structural/functional aspects of e.g., the amygdala, hippocampus or cortical columns. Likewise, knowing about them and not knowing what to do with them other than excising them or injecting some specific medication when injured was not the solution either. We had to develop a hybrid approach combining their respective contributions into one whole unit, the epistemontological unit.

We needed a synthetic a-posteriori modus operandi to be based principally on empirical or contingent results of varying degrees of generality. Our species sense-phenomenal resolution limits under-determine sensory impressions as to their truth value and semantic content. Consequently, the resulting judgments are based on empirical, not a-priori, intuitions. The logical truths of analytic judgments include those possible worlds in which human experience in those noumenal worlds is impossible. Their semantic contents is conceptually, not sensory based. It is important that we learn more about brain dynamics, about how we humans make decisions on important and relevant biopsychosocial (BPS) issues that control the quality of our quotidian and intellectual lives because human rationality is essentially oriented towards making continuous adjustments to optimize the outcomes of our interactivity with changing environmental influences beyond our control. Because of the self-evident biological imperative for the human species survival, as witnessed by the spontaneous, unconscious servo controlled adjustments, our efforts are biased towards an anthropocentric focus sustained primarily by meaningful and trustworthy empirical/referential data inputs. Thus, the emphasis on formulating our judgments based on synthetic a-posteriori propositions especially when analyzing the relevant psychosocial aspects of existence where the results may not necessarily be applicable in all possible worlds. This is not meant to stop the search for universal synthetic a-priori truths as a goal when budgetary priorities are assigned. If nothing else, we unavoidably concluded that beyond sensory phenomena there 'exists' a complex structured reality that resists being reduced to logical representations. All languages explain this as being caused by an 'intelligent design' without being committed to a spatiotemporal description. While natural philosophies are systematically built up on propositions whose bottoms-up inputs originate from directly referential sensory attributions perceptual data, or their conceptualized representations, our innate self-conscious faculties generate a higher order unity that requires the consideration of an 'intelligent design' as history and self-evident negentropic order testifies to. Is there a non-rational or proto-rational consciousness that transcends empirical existential reality? Quare. It was always fun to search and maybe identify the equivalent explanations within the context of biblical Baptist conception of reality which my wife Suzi, an ordained Deaconess, strained to explain as bringing stability and order to most common folks. She had her feet on solid existential reality! She made clear to Quixotic me that windmills cannot substitute for real existential problems.

CHAPTER

12

Many retired colleagues and friends from academia often wonder why anyone like me would insist on continuing to spend precious retired family time trying to explain things like life, consciousness, language acquisition and processing, brain neuronal representations of information and their translation into both inner and reportable language, etc. Is it not better to spend your unpaid time during retirement in sports and entertainment at the golf course or at a bar? Why this almost obsessive, compulsive search for explanations about an invisible world at both ends of an infinity spectrum? Does the mind hallucinate when burdened with a hypothesized overabundant supply of gray matter? I mean also hallucinations on messianic ambitions or on controlling minds for universal or self-serving benefit? I never paid much attention to this slow but unrelenting drive to analyze, scrutinize and forever search for a reason or explanation for anything and everything that moves or not. Or was this all an escape from continuous mental pain sublimized? This is enough to drive anyone normal out of their minds to experience or witness daily. If not, ask my pretty wife, Suzi, always moving around solving her family's unemployment or health problems in perpetual motion along the fast track style of her existence. All of which makes me think about what proportion of doers and thinkers society needs for survival? Can our Volusia County drivers survive without Suzi-like auto mechanics . . . . ? No! Can they survive without Yogi-like experts in classical auto mechanics theory . . . ? Definitely yes! Should people be free to choose their hobbies after retirement? Some choose to be entertained, bar hopping, playing golf, stamp collecting, bed hopping, writing, lawn landscaping, reading, cooking, playing music or travelling. Some choose to be informed as a hobby. What could be wrong with marrying your computer in a joint search for invisible objects to be arbitrarily represented with letters, numbers or words so you can now play with them using also arbitrary and convenient logical rules of play? Should that be considered a hobby or a psychopathological behavior sometimes termed 'sane psychosis'. Should we be saved from enjoyable psychic, indulgent self-destruction . . . . ? Suzi reads, does civic work, writes well when inspired and tends to her flowers, curtains, ducks, egrets, dogs, cats, . . . and me.

I have joined many civic organizations for a long time, Rotaries, Elks, Knights of Columbus, VFW and attend two churches but must confess that my almost exclusive interest was not civic but rather to provide a secure environment for my growing family to socialize. Except that I am considered an antisocial loner where shyness is often confused with conceit until I get past either 2 glasses of Pinot Noir or 2 shots of Haig and Haig Pinch whereupon I join the social group, relax and share my corny German jokes with the yawning, un-interested rest. If I dared to exceed that liquor quota of liver poison, I returned it back to mother earth in convulsive, uncontrollable bouts of oral greenish recursive jet ejections. Then Suzi would drive our Nissan new Altima back home while my head hung outside the car window to inhale fresh air and resuscitate. But before I go to bed I religiously check my computer for exchanges, comments or replies from the Mega International, Omega, Prometheus, Mind and Brain, WedConscious, Ispenet, and other 'one in a million' HiQ listings I participate or monitor, all worldwide groups specializing in all aspects of brain dynamics. All before closing my eyes while giving thanks to my virtual God of choice for all blessings conferred upon me, family and neighbors, nation and earth . . . Not surprisingly, I have to re-read the listings again the next day. Then I find that, e.g., Leon, a brilliant computer engineer, who had been urging me to consider his theological ABC model brain storms as relevant to my interests in developing further my BPS model of consciousness, was dead. I had the urge to reply: "Dear Leon Maurer (now dead), wherever 'you' happen to be now, ... if anywhere., I have been considering your invitation to unite your offer to join your ABC and my BPS models and abandon the quantum theoretical probability interpretation I now follow. I admit that other than modifying a little the Cramer and Walter Freeman's transactional models to accommodate my neocortical pre-motor attractor phase space fixation, I have not been able to cover the details by using micro quantum theory at the Planck level of organization even when my modification is partially rooted on Freeman's brain noise background amplification of sensory signals and subsequent resonant phase coupling with ongoing brain activity. I believe there is enough in quantum theory to justify exploiting its possibilities to adequately represent a reliable picture of thought/language generation that accompany the attainment of the self-conscious state. We may have to invent a new physics to deal with the relatively more reliable measurement of atoms and molecules in fMRI, etc. For example EEG values may represent a spectrum of preferred frequencies varying as does the value of cells membrane's resting voltage and/or ionization potential." What I was trying to tell Leon, the genial mystic, was that we need to spend more time with solving real-time problems here on earth, at the mesoscopic level before we spend all our energies and focus in intergalactic other world's mystical issues. We need not to abandon either the cosmological nor the sub-Planckian invisibilities focus, what we need is to bring those conjectures and speculations to bear more directly into human health, psychic happiness and social conviviality, i.e., pay more attention to the real needs of real people in their pursuit of an individualized, fitting biopsychosocial equilibrium. What this and other considerations suggest to me is that to make sense of it we may need a radical new approach where condensed dark matter, Compton length scales and quantization of Planck constant may have to be considered to bring quantum theory to the macro/mesoscopic level of analysis where it may properly belong. This will allow for a better understanding of how the genetic memory encoded into DNA/RNA influences the activation of unconscious reflex adaptive responses as mediated by the amygdaloidal complex. The 20 A-acids synthesized in response to novel sense phenomenal input may represent the first steps in the production and/ or activation of the relevant membrane receptors in hippocampus where context analysis of the original stimulus takes place. The dark ionic supra currents and their quantum character may be responsible for the phase transitions observed but it would have to be established that the value of Planck constant can be quantized to harmonize it with the observed frequency value range in EEGs. By the way, if you feel I may be dreaming of dark matter instead of a white Christmas or have exceeded my Christmas quota of Pinot Noir or Courvoisier cognac, I will understand! ☺ But one has to pay close attention to dissident expressions because it could indeed be the case that ALL of human knowledge is relational. As, what is cold without heat, light without dark or good without evil? Or as they say, perhaps conscious free will and unconscious determinism, structural/ functional order and random chaos, sense phenomenal and ESP virtual reality, are simply different propositions about the same arguments of scientific logic? As we confidently sense the solidity of an inert gold ring with our fingers science tells us that, not only that a solid ring consists mainly of empty space, but also that inert objects, such as gold rings and rocks, consist of particles whirling round each other trillions of times a second! Likewise, as I have repeated so many times, we are ALL believers in some entity we may want to call God, or not and all may be right, just "traveling the same circle in opposite directions." Because what is God if not a symbolic conceptualization of perfect order and harmony? History has recorded myriad conceptions of God since the dawn of civilization, from the monotheistic God of Judaism and the Trinitarian God of Christians to the nontheistic Buddhism. In fact, the characterization of the same conceptual God of order and perfection comes in all JudeoChrIslamic flavors and yet vary so widely that there's no clear consensus on the definition of the exclusive God that different theologies claim, including materialistic 'atheism' belief in a strictly corporeal (material) world with no afterlife remnant. The classical believers believe God has an incorporeal (immaterial) existence, and that there's an afterlife. As I have repeated many times, my BPS 'epistemontological hybrid model' of existential reality incorporates both material and 'immaterial' aspects as being essentially a co-relative unit. This is another way of saying that "Life and consciousness represents one side of the equation, matter and energy the other." This is not to deny that the current scientific paradigm is properly based on the belief that the world has an objective observer-independent existence, including the human species. But observers we are, only that our sense phenomenal experience as observers of ongoing objects and events depends on our brain, no brain, no reality. We build our understanding of its perceptual and conceptual aspects based on the known limitations of our human species to resolve the details of their noumenal mysteries, a pitiful state of affairs. Consider for example the foundational base of our most successful scientific tools, quantum theory, e.g., the double slit experiment. When you watch radiation particles pass through two slits in a barrier, they go through either one of the slits. But if you don't watch, they go through both slits at the same time. And one may properly ask how can a particle change its behavior depending on whether you are watching it or not? So we invent the waveform as 'representing' the particle to explain the simultaneous passage through the two slits. Just an explanation like Suzi explains what she couldn't witness but it makes some sense when we witness the consequent results of their invisible presence. I still think there is a difference between particles mass—however small—and their attributions, the latter being its mode of propagation as a wave. Who knows? Life is much more than the interactive collisions of some atoms and molecules. Space and time are just convenient tools of the mind to measure observable changes in shape, form, location, etc. of objects/events inside our 4-d existential cage. Likewise, how can their separated quantum-entangled particles appear instantaneously connected on opposite sides of the cosmos as if there's nothing separating them? And how can events in the present effect those in the past? It has even been claimed by scientists that particles sent into an apparatus(?) could retroactively change events that had already happened in the past. One wonders how other species conceive space and time, the properties of matter, life, etc. Does reality mean different things to different observers? Ultimately, is life just autogenous motion and change perceptually intuited but only conceptually comprehensible? But motion is a change in position. The human mind invents the concept of 'time' to measure change and 'space' to measure the displacement from an original position observed. This way, the mind can best understand e.g., the concept of 'velocity' (cm/sec) as uniform displacement in position (cm) every unit of time (seconds). Ditto for non-uniform displacement as in e.g., acceleration seen as a change of velocity (cm/sec) every second. Thus the mind uses relational conceptualization of perceptual events and comes to the intuition of the 'excluded middle', i.e., a perceptual object cannot be and not be at the same time and space. Due to our species perceptual limitations we feel the living presence of relevant entities in our lives that escape sensory detection and thus we intuitively conceive the possibility of an exception to the logic of 'the excluded middle' and thus conceive of the presence of a living, but invisible, God that has provided the foundations for theologies to build on according to their spatio-temporal circumstances. But to some believers God is more than a relational concept product of a complex brain dynamics. For theological believers there is an afterlife. For atheist believers death is the irreversible change/end of any conceivable 'life' as we know it (motion and change of perceptual matter). This self-imposed myopia leaves no room for the possible existence of relevant objects/events that exist below the threshold of perceptual sense detection, e.g., the living survival of invisible condensed matter (below Schwartzchild radius). There is no reason in the world why one should choose to ignore any and all possibilities just because there's has been an evolutionary break in the continuity of space and time upon death. Is it more logical to conceive of a single particle passing through two holes at the same time? Or like 'biocentrists' claim: ". . . you can consider yourself both alive and dead, outside of time". Is this to be considered a logical violation of the law of the excluded middle? Or do we just simply die and rot into the ground while the cosmos continues to tick along like a clock until it reverses its expansion, growing hotter until everything is crushed out of existence in the conceptual possible 'crunch'. This Big Bang/Big Crunch/Big Bang oscillating cycle of 20 billion years duration is part of the Buddhist worldview. The classical view on the conservation of energy in a hypothetical closed system where the resulting increase in the order and complexity of the finished product. i.e., increase in free energy (F) is at the expense of the decrease in the other energy component (-E) of the totality (T) according to T= F + E. Entropy energy (E), besides being equated with an increase in structural/functional disorder it is also considered by some as a transformation into its equivalent matter (M) state according to (M = E/C2) not available now to do work inside the close system but available as an ingredient to a contiguous synthetic component system (a consumer predator somewhat analogous to a link in a food chain where life will continue in the starved predator at the expense of the `dead' prey). This interpretation would be valid if the special consumer-predator is identified. What it means is that we witness the causal chain of linear progression resulting in what seems like a spontaneous increase in organization and complexity (a decrease in the entropy of the system or negentropy) and nowhere to be seen the predicted energy fuel source to drive the counterintuitive increase in complexity. To say that there is a source of energy in an open system is an act of faith just like describing the resulting complexity as being caused by an `intelligent designer', whatever that may be to any observer. This is a logical, and not a theological, argument as many of my detractors argue. In the absence of such physical identification, a metaphysical explanation may do and call the designer =X. In ancient Greece X were Gods of lightning, thunder, etc. Today we jump into the truth train and ride along the asymptotic railway to 'Noumenon' to measure the natural events or simulate them in the lab. As we get closer the dubious/ nebulous certainty of our sensory descriptions soon become the probable and then the possible truth as we struggle with the sentential or symbolic representations that our limited combinatorial brain processor can handle. The asymptotic train trip from the ontological certainty wish station A, epistemological probable/statistical stop theological possible/intuitional stop B, "I give up" final stop describes the genetically-driven human angst in identifying his origins and destination. The serious limitations in our sensory and computational brain hardware pretty much predicts that life will remain an asymptotic journey to 'Noumenon', never reaching that destination. A similar frustration attends our frequent analysis of the 'life' fact. It was not spontaneously produced, as defined in thermodynamic theory for the organization of complex systems. It required a source of external free energy to fuel and sustain physic-chemical reactions resulting in the resultant living organism. It resulted in an increase in structure and complexity of original organic reactants leading to the living organism result. Life cannot be described as a random, blind process according to thermodynamic theory. It was caused, driven by heretofore invariant and unidentified forces responsible for the particularities of the end result. It describes a causal chain of linear progression resulting in a decrease in the entropy of the system (negentropy) environment where such event took place. The eventual structure/functions (of proto-life) are influenced by both genetic and physical/environmental conditions (nature) present where such events took place. The eventual/future structure and function of living descendants (in sexual reproduction) is predicated on parents reaching reproductive maturity and procreating; what we call evolution by natural selection. We can argue that evolution by natural selection (henceforth Mendelian determinism) operates at both the level of the ontogenesis of the individual immediate parents and a recapitulation of the phylogenesis of their descendant(s); what we call evolution by natural selection. Thus, if energy is constant (cannot be created/destroyed) and entropy may be considered a form of energy not available/free to do work, then the total (T) energy may be described as a sum of free energy (F) and entropy (E); $T = F + E$. Consider that when, e.g., heating an egg white there is an expenditure of external energy as the egg proteins denature and become tangled, that is also explained in classical physics as the transformation of the viscous, amorphous liquid egg white into a structured solid with a determined dimension and shape requiring heat energy to attain that particularized end configuration. This is an endergonic process, arguably just like creating a particularly beautiful solid statue from an amorphous viscous cement pile requiring the energy and imagination of the creative artist. It is argued both processes would still require additional 'energy' to further change their configuration, e.g., a push from the window to reduce the statue to rubble or a grinder to reduce the solid egg white to a mush (not the original viscous egg white). What seems common to both examples before is that the energy of the window push or the grinder was required only when my design in mind is executed according to my free willed/desired goal (intelligent or not). Left to themselves, both the statue and the solid egg white will never spontaneously become another statue or special gourmet egg white respectively, both will inexorably, with the passage of time and in the absence of any intelligent designer, alter nature's course, and will become dust. This describes a spontaneous exergonic process whose temporal evolution is determined by the particular/restrictive environmental processes present, because ALL systems observed in nature tend to be minimums of free energy state. Ergo, if we agree as to the self-evident, historically verified. evolved order in the structure/ function and complexity of social institutions, and if we agree as to the observed/ documented order in the evolution of structure/function and complexity in the cosmological domain, and if we agree as to the undeniable structural/functional super-complexity of living species during their ontogenetic/phylogenetic evolution into living systems, then we have to agree, as per preceding honest stipulations, that the order and complexity we witness as time passes, cannot be spontaneous. Instead, they are examples of an endergonic process directed to an unknown end or recurrent cyclic stage(s) beyond our present cognitive capacities to precise/describe or even explain. Ergo, the preceding is consistent with the unexplained physical or metaphysical presence of an intelligent 'designer' whose symbolic/sentential logical representation is up for grabs depending on one's level of intellectual sophistication, genetic, memetic biases, emotions, experiences and other circumstantial variables. All organic matter found in living systems is the result of endergonic reactions because it required external energy expenditures to fuel their structured conversion and comes from photosynthesis or activated chemistry reactions. The breathing of life into such organic matter is a different story. But that doesn't mean that positive mutational changes and the consequent selective evolution by natural selection are simply 'endergonic', not to mention their being 'blind', or 'random' especially when the 'blind' selection results in a more structured and complex-in-function entity. These negentropic results are not spontaneous in any physic-mathematical system we know of. The self-evident increase in complexity witnessed is always an endergonic process that cannot be always credibly explained as happening at the expense of the immediate environment decrease in energy (exergonic). We need to escape this vicious cycle/oscillation evolution ÅÆ intelligent design by either changing our physical laws (thermodynamics) to accommodate metaphysical causality or declaring our human species limitations in ever achieving cognitive certainty. Next best is a probable, best adaptive explanation (model) we can live with and in harmony with our biological, psychic and social needs, whether genetically and/or memetically-driven. Perhaps we should concentrate more on the analysis of the mesoscopic level of existential reality without ever abandoning the informed search for better inferential explanations of relevant objects/events beyond our limited sensory detection/description. Sorry for the 'leit motif'. As I get wiser and older I no longer feel there is an absolute need to identify noumenal dynamics because it would require an infinite resolution in sense perceptual capacity and an infinite brain capacity to represent and parse all relevant but invisible variables likely to be encountered, i.e., absolute truth is a necessary but unreachable goal for our human species. Inevitably, this unavoidable skepticism forces us to be content with accepting a reality that is consistent with such perceptual and conceptual limitations. Thus. one must settle for a dynamic, hybrid existential reality consistent with short-sighted goals of a healthy, solvent and happy life, which ultimately I reduce to a transient moment in time where biological, psychic and social equilibrium is maintained. As you know, by training we feel committed to root our conclusions on good measurements and good mathematical logic to compensate for invisible but relevant factors present. That self-imposed discipline makes us deterministic and teleologically oriented as to causality; that is the reason I have spent 4 book volumes in doing just that. Unfortunately for those in search for ultimate truths, the biological imperative that sustains and protects the living by neuro-humoral mediation will always bias, if not control, our decision-making process no matter how hard we try to be exclusively objective. Reality is always subjective because it finds its meaning inside our hardware/software-limited dynamic physical brain. Emotions play a fundamental role in this life-preserving activity, and is much more than the result of inter-synaptic, neuro-humoral receptor activity. Neuro-humoral activity at receptor sites is only the ontological aspect of the existential reality hybrid.

To illustrate, in the Florida recent murder case trial against Casey Anthony, the media frenzy and the public outrage on the verdict is predicated on their ignorance that all it means is that Casey's guilt could not be established factually, even though she may have in fact committed the crime. This very distinction ontological/factual and epistemo-logical/inferential reality is what separates the physical reductionist and the existential realist that must go on for what is reasonably probable and not politically viable. I chose to do an experiment with myself while listening to both closing arguments. Already on the first week of testimony I had an intuitive feeling, based on clues from Casey's body language expressions, that she couldn't have formed the conscious, intentional 'mens rea' to kill her biological child. That was confirmed based on evidence presented and verdict. But, the prosecution arguments were also credible at closing arguments and I felt stupid—as a licensed lawyer—in realizing that moment's conclusion that both opposing narratives were probably true! But then I recuperated when I also realized this was not about absolute truth and certainty but about probable truth, all things considered. We pitiful humans . . . .

CHAPTER

13

It is impossible not to feel frustrated about how much time I have spent looking for human answers to unanswerable questions. I have almost completed a lifetime cycle of search for answers to the question of existence, life and conscious free will; that slow, hesitant but unrelenting trip to experience noumenal truth only to end where I started with nothing much to share to advance the cause of humanity. But evolutionary advances, albeit very slow, have definitively been historically recorded.

Suzi looks at me with pitiful eyes as if saying "the more things change, the more they remain the same." It is my retirement hobby to follow the drum beats of an internal voice guiding my search . . . "For what?", Ms. Suzi 'Sancho Panza' replies to a saddened Don Quixote that continues his relentless battle with the windmills (human species limitations) thinking they are the super complexities of existence that need solution. We will probably never know for sure but it's fun to at least guess the probability of an occurrence based on our reasoned speculations and conjectures. "Yes, but how have all those predictions improved on the basic animal behavior of the human species?" Suzi argues, "human relations are even worse even here in the U.S.A." No doubt she has a good point. Should we all become Sartrean existentialists and live from crisis to crisis? We cannot even trust our own introspective self-searches for reliable data on which to base our decisions. Are we all 'aka dummies' looking at ourselves in the mirror and believing the reflection we 'see'? Is absolute, introspective self-knowledge an illusion? Suzi knew that for the next hours I would be lost in reflective activity and she would lose my company again. The Spanish philosopher Ortega y Gasset's dictum that humans cannot ever divorce themselves from their ongoing biopsychosocial (BPS) circumstance ("El hombre es el y su circumstancia.") posits for me one of the most intriguing questions about human behavior when confronted with real-time, relevant existential, ongoing contingencies during the decision-making process. Which aspect controls the resulting decision? Can the self always rely on knowing the absolute truth value? If our human species proudly claim being the protagonists of a neo-Copernican revolution that situates us at the very center of the universe because of being uniquely endowed with the marvel of being able to report on a conscious, introspective journey into ourselves, then it is proper to investigate the expected invariance of that solid knowledge base supporting our decision-making activity when confronting and solving contingencies threatening our lives or biopsychosocial equilibrium. The successful evolution of the species depends on the solidity of our self-knowledge base so we do not evolve, like other species, as mere creatures of changing circumstances. How is a real-time human being going to find that quotidian solution that is both simultaneously relevant, adaptive and at the same time, transcending its immediate immanent character to become the absolute standard of righteousness independent of any variations in the circumstantial aspects surrounding the specific individualized contingency? From the perspective of a universal standard, can our human species escape his circumstantial shadow that inexorably follows him regardless of his conscious awareness of its possibly negative impact presence? If we were to trust recorded history accounts, only a few individuals successfully resisted the convenience drive of his biopsychosocial circumstance and opted, 'contra natura', to swim against the strong current and altruistically act against self-interest conveniences to set universal standards of behavior for others to emulate in the Ten Commandments Decalon, Tables of the Law, Koran, etc. We call them the historical prophets. What guided them? Where is their source of inspiration and guidance? How is righteousness transformed into a living reality? Informed speculations and conjectures are thus in order to at least answer the how, e.g., the highly speculative BPS sub-model of Reciprocal Transcendental Information Transfer between the human neo cortex and transfinity. At this time, I find it necessary to further expand briefly on the nature of the complex question being asked. Why are some humans in history 'more special" than others connecting with that mysterious 'source' regardless of their preceding formal training in ethics, axiology, etc? In the following explanation, I will try an objective analytical perambulatory dissection of this issue on how we gain and use knowledge.

One can gain ontological knowledge about the immediate external world and internal body-proper phenomenal environment with the aid of instrumental recordings from external receptors as in vision, audition, taste, touch, temperature, etc. or with internal proprioceptors, stretch receptors, muscle spindles, chemoreceptors, etc. We establish their ontological status by the more reliable direct measurements of their structure/function or the less reliable spoken accounts/ reports or explanations of the subjective qualia experienced. Phenomenologically, these real time, ongoing descriptions entail a minimal form of self-conscious activity for the experiencing subject due to the immediacy of the object or event being witnessed or otherwise experienced. But, even when we are asked, immediately after the occurrence, to give an account of what happened, how do we know that one's ongoing, particular mental state, beliefs, desires, sensations, etc. did not significantly influence our reply? That particular/exclusive mental state is very important. It happens to be our persisting self, our personality, our identity as quoted by the classical Greeks as 'Gnoscete Ipsum' or 'know thyself.' But, is an 'objective' ontological description being modified by 'subjective' epistemological explanations controlled by our immediate and ongoing mind state or a persisting mental state? What controls the decision-making process, convenient short term expediency or long term ethical and moral universal considerations? Is our 'self-knowledge' data base persistent or subject to expedient and convenient modifications? Phrased differently, is the decision-making process controlled by an introspective, conscious self-knowledge or by the subconscious genetic and memetic reflex networks? It is the role of the subconscious neuro-humoral control network to provide the necessary adjustments responsible for the biopsychosocial (BPS) equilibrium servo controls, those that make possible for human beings to reflexly respond to familiar situations as recorded in their memory data base. New unfamiliar situations mobilize additional self-conscious resources that make it possible to adapt to the potentially dangerous novelty on the basis of either BPS needs or conveniences, immanent or transcendental aspirations and rarely, altruistic acts against self-interests. There is a very important distinction to be made between knowledge acquired through perceptual familiarity and knowledge acquired by conceptual representations, i.e., knowledge we describe with some certainty and knowledge we explain by way of inferential symbolic or sentential logical representations of both physical and non-physical properties. When we make normative logical decisions about the relevant non-physical, extra sensory invisibilities, it is only when they are rooted on the falsifiable, measurable and probable facts about objects and/or events that we can claim to be speaking with a Kantian wisdom, a sort of epistemological naturalism or epistemontological. A reading of Kant's Critique of Pure Reason will explain it better. When the human experience to be communicated resist statistical apprehension by Bayesian logic, we are now in a very different but equally important psychosocial theological manifold which humans individually adopt as our living truths in harmony with their evolving individualized, real time existential circumstance. As we can see, there are many layers in the content of that self- knowledge reservoir we tap when making conscious, freely willed decisions. We hope the reader differentiates this time honored, historically recorded, self evident truths from the typical Sartrean existentialism where individuals live and blindly evolve from moment to moment with no normative guidelines to show the righteous way to behave to preserve the viability of the human species. However, the self -evident truth is that we, as a species, have evolved in obvious defiance to the also self-evident and reliable natural thermodynamic laws of entropy. Why? Why do some people lead lives exemplifying moral virtues, prudence and courage, benevolence and compassion notwithstanding the many and various temptations to look exclusively after their own ego centered self-interests often at the expense of innocent others, like so many currently elected or appointed politicians? Egoism comes in different flavors—psychic, rational or a deadly combination of both when it evolves into a normative rational mindset where the ultimate aim is to unrelently maximize one's self-interest at any cost. A veritable intentional psychopathological state of the likes of Hitler, Stalin, Franco, Napoleon and other brilliant historical non-repentant personalities; these are the diametrical opposites of our historical prophets. If these diametrically opposite extremes of historical behavior are conditioned by natural inherited intelligence and not the result of a corresponding circumstantial existential reality, what then is the fundamental difference? In the classical 'Summa Contra Gentiles' it is suggested that through 'divine assistance' some chosen individuals are blessed with a direct and immediate grasp of first principles. This reminds us again to ponder on the nature of that claimed divine assistance as being essentially the ability to harmonize the unavoidable, immanent self BPS interests with the transcendental and universal requirements of virtuosity; like Leibniz conceptualization of theology as a human brain centered effort in the 'chosen ones' to create a "science of law". It is almost impossible for us limited human creatures to conceive of an 'assistance', divine or not, as lacking an efficient physical cause, however small in dimensions. Therein lies the mesmerizing attraction of an epistemology rooted primarily on functional reality as experienced, e.g., the Kantian 'synthetic a priori propositions'; also somewhat reminiscent of Locke's faith on what material substances and their powers can do outside our capability of ever measuring their dimensions or functions. But we can always write about the explanatory poetry of a belief or just muse on sheer 'cult' nonsense. Been there, done that. After all, why deny it, human certainty is nothing but an epistemic property of human subjects communicating their beliefs with the assistance of all kinds of convenient metaphysical logic and other axiomatic contraptions, however practically useful they may turn out to be. For those of us addicted with the curiosity for the identification of noumenal reality or first principles, we have no choice but to rely on the self evident truth that drives our belief-forming activities. Unfortunately. the best guide we humans have is what appears to us as counter intuitive, e.g., those non-physical epistemological conceptualizations that become entities able to produce forces that affect physical objects or events. Last but not least, the Darwinian evolution abstraction may be the result of indirect interpretations about observations but it sure as hell makes sense to speculate, if not believe, that species do change in appearance due to what seems to be a natural process that 'selects and maintains' in nature. This may be necessary to explain how species change but may not be sufficient to explain ALL BPS changes experienced inside our quotidian 4d real time existential cage. 'Evolutionary epistemology' is in! We have to live with it until a better epistemological poetry explanation comes into being, especially when analyzing the 'replication' pathway of the selected change. Spontaneously self-sustained? If so, we may have to change all of our physics laws that have been so successful in predicting the probability of future events because they do not predict a spontaneous increase in complexity of structure or function as we corroborate as happening in recorded history. Finally, it is very tempting to assume that acquiring and reporting knowledge about the external environment shouldn't be different when doing the same in respect to ourselves because, if we accept the premise that reality is in our brains, why go elsewhere? But we have to keep looking and continue to write poetry. We can summarize and easily conclude that there is no doubt that most of us humans rely blindly on our introspective memory accounts of our respective lives because they seem infallible and seem to account for at least all of our acquired existential knowledge. The rest of our knowledge is in genetic data bases we cannot change at will. After all, it seems odd that we should feel that what we are thinking about in any given moment is not true! Yet, how can we be certain we are capable of attaining a third person perspective about our self-attributions, free from higher order inferences adopted from prefab 'theories of mind' or behavioral influences? Even Dr. Dennet agrees but calls it differently. Interestingly, we have analyzed (see articles on intra and interspecies information transfer) how we may be utilizing same brain circuitry, especially mirror neurons, in gaining reliable insights about our own mental states as we do in others' mental states. In this simulation effort we may learn of other's states of mind by using their facial expression cues in a given situation and then projecting oneself empathically into the other's situation, i.e., allowing the observer through a special mode of self-reflection, to experience what one would believe or desire, feel, etc. if we were in that situation ourselves. We had hoped to use similar arguments to explain how the use of similar brain processing circuitry may be activated when receiving information from transfinity sources, if any. We have argued that this 'simulation theory certainty' needs to be qualified and improved on. When we are asked to report on our personal account of, e.g., an accident we had just witnessed, how many persons may 'consciously' report relevant objects, events or sensations 'experienced' but not strictly present inside our perceptual field or emotional mindset during the occurrence? Was it influenced by the reporter's current and ongoing mindset or was it objective even when it would carry negative consequences to the reporter or to his special others? Why the inconsistency? Is this the result of the inevitable subconscious influence from individualized circumstances, e.g., sensations, emotions, appetites, etc. or was it always the result of a conscious deliberate intention to benefit from the consequences? Are we really having those thoughts and sensations reported? Are they true? There is no unanimous consensus as to how to evaluate the results of introspective reports, or what weight to accord 'other sources'. Introspection therefore faces an especially complex problem of "standard of calibration." Should we rely on what often seems to be an exalted epistemic claim made on behalf of introspective self-consciousness as being true and very distinct from the brain epistemic processing we use in other domains, i.e., on what credible basis can we claim that there is a fundamental difference between self-knowledge and other-knowledge? What is obviously distinct is the leisurely, scholarly, addictive habit of the few retired to indulge in poetry writing about the complexities of self and the many others sharing the same ecological niche, very different from the quotidian existential reality of the surviving, unemployed and stressed 'many others' coexisting with us. Nothing wrong with writing poetry so long as you keep your feet on the solid grounds of real time existence as you look at the stars for guidance and then take the first step 'ad astra per asperas'.

Suzi calmly observes with innate curiosity how I strain to explain what is not even clear to me as I step down from the clouds into the high horses and then get my feet on solid ground where real-time existence continues unfazed, "time to eat honey." And then, back to existential reality . . . . For example, how can anyone escape the anguish of witnessing how death lurked in my two older sons' lives? Why not hypothetically become their friends instead of a loving father that has not left a stone unmoved trying to prevent the inevitable? I need to keep living . . . so I tried.

CHAPTER 14

What is the difference between friendship and love? After having experienced the hurt associated with the loss of her son and husband before she met me, Suzi will understand, I hope, the oddity of my escaping into metaphysical explanations to rationalize my solution to find inner peace and keep going. Bear with me Suzi . . . The hurtful experience of witnessing the painful journey of my son from a moribund state into the irreversible death and transfiguration, and the concomitant expressions of empathy and love from friends and family everywhere, gave me the opportunity to reflect further on the co-existence of both abstract metaphysical and practical existential aspects of transcultural love and friendship as recently identified in the various expressions of condolences from family and friends worldwide, all now briefly analyzed below from a biopsychosocial perspective. Because of the wide trans-cultural spectrum, ranging from my readers whom I have never personally met to biological filiations, I am trying, myself, to understand if friendship and love qualia may be an essential part of the inherited and/or acquired survival instinct or does it transcend the primitive function of keeping the human species together for the common defense against survival threats or against their collective biopsychosocial integrity in order to guarantee the survival and continuation of the species to reproductive age and beyond. Or is it part and parcel of another metaphysical, impersonal, apathetic logical elaboration of the language faculty that expresses a ratification of value and commitment to defend universal values and entities as varied as other species, objects, principles or goals? This metaphysical language processing tend to conceptualize into analytical, abstract, symbolic and sentential representations (metaphors) of the real time existential experience of the grieving actor (whether inherited, acquired and 'revealed') which will stoically and dispassionately bear on his decision-making processes to rationalize the painful quale when accessed. Does it express an abstract but genuine love or an equally genuine existential friendship? Is there a difference? Do we need to choose or do we consciously will, as an adaptive defense mechanism, an ataraxic state to mediate but inevitably execute a compromise between the ontologically, existentially experienced angst and the epistemologically, rationally idealized in abstraction? Before I proceed further in this brief analysis, I need to explain what is the western cultural norm for describing existential love. Quoting from 1 Cor. 13:4-7, NIV, Apostle Paul described love in the famous poem in 1 Corinthians, thus: "Love is patient, love is kind. It does not envy, it does not boast, it is not proud. It is not rude, it is not self-seeking, it is not easily angered, it keeps no record of wrongs. Love does not delight in evil but rejoices with the truth. It always protects, always trusts, always hopes, and always perseveres." It is self-evident this metaphysical universal-laden quote does not describe the behavior of most of us mortal members of the human species. This kind of conscious impersonal behavior is drawing heavily from both coexisting, neutrally valence-coded brain data bases. One wonders what guides a human being to preferentially transcend his pitiful real time human existence and accordingly learn also to objectively love those objects, principles, or goals they value greatly, like Suzi does with all animals and plants. Can one deeply commit oneself to their defense and preservation even when it is possibly threatening their own preservation, e.g., like the historical prophets or the present-day conservationists? This is to be distinguished from the essentially subjective, emotional, consciously interpersonal bonding outreach of some volunteers with e.g., objects, political or spiritual convictions, animals, etc. This should not be confused with psychopathological cases of paraphilia where sexual delusions become part of the subject's mindset. We have all experienced the interpersonal expressions of love at the ontological level as essentially a biological human effort, not very different from the extinction of hunger or thirst driven by neuro-hormones and characterized by probable sexual attraction and attachment. The latter is better characterized as the psycho-social and cultural acquired component influenced also in its instantiation or embodiment by hormones promoting an experience of mental well-being, e.g., oxytocin, vasopressin, neuro-trophins, pheromones, etc. The signs and symptoms of this physiological arousal are characterized by transitory, trivial cardio-respiratory dysfunction. An important variation of this interpersonal element is that seen when the epistemological component is in control, i.e., where the experience of affectionate feeling of intimacy and empathy is not accompanied by physiological arousal. Is the emotional component totally absent? Quare. When my international friends from HiQ listings and extended distant family that I have not seen or heard from for a long time send cards and e-mails of condolences, do they truthfully say what they mean and mean what they say or is it just a culturally-imposed, emotionally-neutral protocol/language script being followed? Interestingly, in my mental perambulations in search of tranquility and adequacy of response to suffering, I discovered the Pyrrhonians epistemological approach most convenient because the situation could be handled in theory as an impersonal relation. Why assume the love expressions from the stranger are not truly qualia experienced by the sender? I have often discussed with Suzi about the qualia truthfulness of birthday cards scripts. Why not suspend judgment on dogmatic cultural or theological beliefs in the absence of factual evidence or credible intuitions? But more important, one can rationalize the situation and ask the Epicureans question, "Why should I worry about an intention I do not even know exists?" This was the same type of rational liberation from the anguish of the unknown I managed to experience when viewing the dying scenario of my son before my teary eyes, a sort of conscious self-induced tranquil apatheia as long as I have no rational way to establish either the physical torment of my dead son or the truth of the intentions of the condolence senders. In retrospect, if I have consistently acted with respect, consideration, praised the trustworthy, being compassionate and affectionate with dissenting colleagues and friends, and consciously have practiced virtuosity (most of the times ☺), why should I worry? If I have consciously behaved that way, I need not be concerned about the valence of love and friendship of others as long as I am able to love and be a good, friendly sentient being. This conscious, tranquil mental state is described by the Greeks as the 'ataraxic' state. Is this the functional role of the metaphysical, logic-based, universally valued metaphor abstractions that the language faculty codes for our human species to "consciously" access when in need to search for an adaptive BPS tranquil state, however immanent and transient? In closing, a note to my local and international friends, family and colleagues: Please accept my sincere thanks for your cards, phone calls and e-mails offering your condolences for the untimely death of our beloved sons. Your thoughtfulness will be long remembered. I hope Suzi understands my questioning of commercial scripts to be found in commercial cards. What is important is that it coincides with your true feelings and if not, you become committed to try to live up to the written expressions you adopted, so help you God. I promise I will have one more account of how I was able to rationalize my painful experiences to save my mental self from inner self destruction because love is a "saber" with two sharp cutting edges.

CHAPTER

Rationalizing life & existence to escape painful qualia. Death and Transfiguration Once I had survived the ineffable experience of being a living witness of the untimely death and transfiguration of my two loving, older sons, the only way I knew to keep going was to escape suffering and frustration by fantasizing reality as my close friends and family describe it. I know of no other way to escape the pain that started as soon as I was able to distinguish self from others. Bear with me again in this last chapter. We, as individuals, seem to be controlled by two, often disparate, existential systems, each endowed with its own distinct strategy when processing the idea of life and the circumstance of quotidian, real time existence and death. Both existential mind sets, conscious and subconscious, respectively, can significantly change our behavioral handling of unexpected contingencies such as actually coming face to face with impending death and suffering as was my case. The epistemological/ abstract eternal and the ontological/individualized experiential, clash in both attitudes and actions as the will, many times, works out adaptive solutions in very different—almost opposite—ways. The coexistence of both conscious and subconscious strategies comes dramatically into life when experiencing and/or witnessing the metaphysical and emotional evolution of a human death experience.

I have been obsessed about life and consciousness for as long as I have been able to think. Here is a short chronology of how now, at the sunset of my productive life, I have almost completed a full cycle and I repeat, the more essential things change, the more they remain almost the same for us pitiful humans. Life. At the risk of being repetitious I still remember many years back, when I was a young Catholic biophysicist at Sloan-Kettering Institute for Cancer Research, I was very curious about how a white crystalline ribonucleic acid (RNA) powder (Rous Sarcoma Virus or RSV) standing in a test tube for weeks could come 'alive' when cultured with chick embryo fibroblasts cells in culture. I couldn't wait to capture and describe for my doctoral thesis that crucial moment of life animation by recording serial measurements with the latest biophysical chemistry technology including electron microscopy. Then I was lost and threw in the towel as my Rous Sarcoma Virus disappeared from inside the cellular cytoplasm. What happened to the electron microscope? The huge electron microscope seemed to 'apologize' to anxious me. Soon afterwards RSV was found by somebody else to have incorporated itself into the fibroblast cell host nuclear DNA. And soon afterwards Howard and Temin won a Nobel Prize by describing how an RNA transcriptase enzyme enabled the viral replication based on similar results. At that time, I simply called the RSV crystal a 'truncated life' who hijacked the host cell's reproductive machinery for its own cancerous replicating ends. I then decided to come back to that 'life enigma', in a neurophilosophical broader context upon retirement. Today, after four published volumes and a 'Treatise' on a model of brain dynamics, the problem has become more complex than I had bargained for, as will be briefly discussed below. The main Gordian knot has been an unnecessary quest by physical scientists and metaphysical theologians alike for a monadic interpretation of life at the exclusion of the other. Our contribution has been to argue for what's worth on both sides of the same coin. Scientific methodology has failed to explain how life, albeit in apparent or presumed abeyance of the first and second law of thermodynamics, is able to spontaneously evolve into a complex structural and dynamic entity able to self-generate and sustain a super-complex intrinsic order; all allegedly without the benefit of a preceding blueprint for such specific destiny. The fundamental transition from inorganic/organic atoms and molecules into a living unit of life still remains a fundamental mystery in physics, chemistry, and biology because of a lack of empirically complete and consistent descriptions or explanations of life as an emergent, irreducible and animated fact of nature, including Dr. Dennet's . . . and my own of course for that matter. One can understand why the comfort of giving some rest to an unsatisfied inquiring mind by resting the case on a convenient "self-replicating" DNA which understandably has evolved into a major metaphor for explaining all there is to be learned about life. After all, why not invoke coding self-replicators and coded self-organizing interactors at all levels of organization to evasively counteract the inescapable and self-evident causally efficient but invisible driving force which seems to be controlling evolution by natural selection? However, it is just as counter-intuitive to analytical logic to conceptualize humans as survivalist epiphenomenal gene-vehicles, a la Dawkins or Dennet, as it is to invoke the exclusive mediation of an intelligent design force or blueprint guiding such beautiful and complex order defying natural laws as witnessed in developmental and evolutionary biology. What IS life then? Let's first agree on the terminology. What do we mean by 'life', 'existence', 'essential' as opposed to 'accidental' attributions, and other ambiguities. Having personally witnessed the early death and transfiguration of my dear son John Arthur, I had the opportunity to differentiate between that conceptualized instant of animation of matter when 'life' comes into being, like the RSV ribonucleoprotein described above, and that subsequent, perceptual description of 'life in transit' that I chose to call 'existence' in real time. Central to 'life' is its scientific characterization of 'existence' as essentially open-ended systems yet subtly maintained in steady states and yet far from an equilibrium, all sustained by a self-regulated inflow/outflow of matter/energy to fuel self-regulated auto-catalytic smaller cycles. The latter are somehow programmed to complete a much larger human life cycle of simultaneously conjoined endergonic negentropy and exergonic entropy. In the beginning of the cycle—the endergonic control phase—we sense and respond to internal and external environments, we extract energy, build and generate complex sub-systems at a faster rate than at a later exergonic control phase where we degrade energy, deconstruct and degenerate at faster rates as we complete our human cycle of life, happiness, suffering and eventual death. Living is dying, but only for the individual. The species continues to evolve. As we learn more and more about the biophysical chemistry of living organisms, we seem to be in denial that, because we cannot ontologically describe either a causally efficient force to drive the dynamics of the living or the essential negentropy of structural/functional details of its self-evident order, there must exist an epistemological metaphysical entity providing the blueprints for their orderly evolution into a living unit. So, why not ignore those two postulates of scientific methodology and invoke the mysterious existence of autopoietic, self generating, self-sustaining, super-complex activity that, equally mysteriously 'emerges' into a super-complex living unit? As such, that miracle of creation is seen as being somehow essentially endowed with another super-complex genetic and memetic memory database good for a human life cycle, a materialistic act of faith and denial. So much for the super-complexity of the enactment of life from the non-living. What about the evolutionary path of the living unit as it unfolds in real space-time? Do we evolve according to the exclusively rational ontological model of the materialistic faith or the exclusively epistemological model of the theological faith? What kind of decision-making behavior, should we predict from either model? Are there other alternatives? Stay tuned for a rehash of the same, all explained and crunched into less than a thousand pages, an epistemontological model of conscious reality. See also Harold 2001. It has not been so bad for an ontological scientific model of 'life' rooted essentially on falsifiable sense-phenomenal measurements on the one hand and intuitions about experiences on invisible and significant objects and/or events whose existential meaning is epistemologically found when expressed and communicated in a metaphysical logic language, on the other hand, a hybrid model of sorts. But which side of the epistemontological coin do we choose? Do we need to have choices? Existence. contrary to the experience of the originally elongated chick embryo fibroblast that predictably got transformed into a spherical tumor cell within the standard environmental temperature and pressure condition (STP) of the experiment, in the exclusive case of the human species, existence is an individualized, self-conscious experience of being oneself. This is distinct from the relevant sense-phenomenal or intuited invisible surroundings which become the human existential circumstance. Yet we are inseparably joined together in most cases. The human existence is predicated on inherited, acquired or willfully (or not) created circumstances. The latter does not exclude circumstances from being consciously willed (or not) as imaginary, mythical, fictional, and the like. To say that it 'exists' means/ implies it is 'real' for a self-conscious person within a stated probability. If the object/event is a pathognomonic reality of mental disease it is not proper to say it 'exists'. If something 'is', whether ontologically sensed or epistemologically inferred as probable (not possible!) under specified STP conditions, then it 'exists' under the scrutiny of metaphysical logic methods even if invisible to the sensory detection. In other words, existence implies a probable predicate attribution of an entity that 'is', ontologically measured matter or an epistemologically inferred micro mass because of extrasensory dimensions. It is important to distinguish further between the existential—as defined—and the predicative context. There is an essential and an accidental predicate. A particulate matter is an essential predicate—invisible or not to human detection—whereas a wave form is an accidental predicate expressing the manner in which the particulate matter travels in space time. Color, shape, etc. are examples of accidental, non-essential predicates. Of more common use are, unfortunately, identity predicates where equivalent essential or accidental features are substituted for the original and then the representation handled as if they 'existed' in reality and not analogically, a serious categorical error often found in the literature. Thus man is essentially a genetically determined biological entity with environmentally determined, acquired accidental predicates such as temperament, color, stature, and other psychosocial attributions. It should be obvious that once there exist accidental predicates there's got to be an implied essential predicate because the former cannot have an independent existence. "Man" is he and his circumstance, a truly biopsychosocial (BPS) hybrid with free will. Without an introspective self-consciousness-based free will, one can conceive of a BPS adapted sub-human living being whose behavior or decision making process can be explained by Skinnerian operant conditioning or simulated in a computer. It is both the introspective capacity and the consequent co-generation of a silent proto language and thought that is exclusively human, as argued elsewhere. Having outlined the primacy of the genetically driven biological imperative of self-preservation under unconscious control as an essential predicate and the memetically driven accidental predicate of his psychosocial existential circumstances under subconscious control, we should be in a position to generalize a model predicting the decision-making process for the human species. Which aspect will carry more weight in the free willing of behavioral adaptive alternatives, the rational or the emotional? Both, in most cases. The human species has been able to transcend the coded alternatives programmed in his genetic and memetic data bases and improvise a very individualized adaptive response tailored to his ongoing existential circumstance at that particular instance, sometimes contrary to his own BPS interests. When you objectively ponder on this scenario, you will realize that the materialistic, physicalist approach rooted exclusively on scientific methodology, while necessary and persuasive, is not sufficient to adequately model the dynamics of life and existence. We need to complement the physical evolutionary approach with a metaphysical component that will reach outside our 4-d space time for answers as explored in one of our dissertations. Of course, one can always settle for a myopic invocation of the magic of multiple auto-poetic, self generated and self sustained forces that magically and spontaneously 'emerge' into a super complexity that violates the very physico-mathematical foundations of the physicalist rational approach. What role do non-rational, emotional circumstances play in the survival of our human species?

What follows was my deliberate, non-classic way of dealing with powerful emotions that threatened to control my life, like a family death can, Death and Transfiguration. As my teary eyes watched my son Johnny die I kept asking myself when does life end? Does life refer more to the functional integrity of the metabolic machinery sustaining the vital homeostatic processes like cell respiration and generation or does it mean the sudden or gradual extinction of that integrated 'animation' of matter we normally describe as being 'alive'? For most of us parents, it is more like experiencing an irreversible harrowing process where both aspects exist, the biological chronicle of 'systems failure' and the sudden extinction of all measurable indices of animation. The former is described by the physical credo that models the scientific physicalist script, the latter is explained by the metaphysical script that models the theological credo. This inextricable duality makes life and death impossible to disambiguate. Having accepted death as a permanent, irreversible event, it now looks like the virtual mirror image of birth and life is seen now as 'something' that moves in and out of matter. But we may synthesize complex matter in the laboratory but never living/animated matter as described above. The combination of both sex gametes' DNA at fertilization to 'synthesize' living matter has always required a living cellular environment. Perhaps we will never know how 'life' was carried or induced at conception. As I pondered and grieved, I turned my focus on the comparative effects of this ongoing process of the dying, and myself on two levels. The first level was an evaluation of the efficacy of interspecies information transfer between Johnny and me. The second level was a speculation as to his suffering vis-a-vis my own. It did not take long for me to realize that the un-natural analgesic and anxiolytic pharmacological effects on both observed and observer respectively would seriously interfere with our cortical pre-motor mirror neurons and limbic systems as amply discussed elsewhere in one of my books. When he was still in denial of the seriousness of his condition, his facial musculature profile and mental alertness reflected his hopes for recovery. When he was close to death his facial musculature relaxed as his mindscape revealed confusion and/or acceptance of his condition; at one point he even smiled as I broke down in tears. Not being able to analyze much at the first level, I turned into a speculation as to whether towards the end he was still suffering at least as much as I did. I was surprised at what a self-induced rationalization of the ongoing experience can do. At that point, it became much clearer the distinction between the unconscious, subconscious and introspective self-consciousness aided by the co-generation of silent language and thought. I re-discovered, as hinted in a previous publication, that ultimately, rationalization of existential reality is a self-serving activity geared to provide an experience of biopsychosocial well-being, an epicurean hedonistic goal!! Following are the tentative arguments I fashioned in my head inside the Hospice room on that Sunday before my handsome dear Johnny finally died.

Nobody wants their lives to end unless in agonizing pain, not the case of Johnny. But 'it' can move in at birth and out of existence at death, i.e. if there is re-incarnation, life is like an intervening gap of non-instantiated hibernation, and death is a sort of break from 'existence' in the real, dangerous world and will continue in a paradisiac sleep state waiting for a subsequent second or third coming . . . Epicurus is smiling in his animated hibernation! Epicurus characterized death as a harrowing evil but then rationalized: "to whom?" Not to Johnny. Death will not affect him because when alive it is absent and when it comes, he is absent. For death to harm the subject who dies, there must exist a subject who is harmed by death to satisfy its causal efficiency. Furthermore, who can precise the nature of the harm and the time and place where that harm is materialized? Restating, when the subject is alive there is no death and after we die there is no living subject to be harmed. Ergo, grief is entirely self-centered. I, the father, who wrapped myself inside a blanket of self-pity and guilt, emotionally grieve at my possible indirect, un-intentional involvement in his demise. But Johnny's body and mind are not harmed by its own extinction. If we ponder hard and find out we did everything a parent can do to preserve his life, we can be harmed only by whatever real negative deeds that will cause us or others to suffer. Is this the unavoidable, self-serving or self-preserving BPS integrity function of self-consciousness, to rationalize an escape hatch and survive as a species? We have examined in detail how humans can logically analyze a situation in abstract, with the best of our analytical faculties during a decision-making contingency, only to find out how the individualized, ongoing, real time existential reality hijacks the logical justifications in providing the subject with a feeling of biopsychosocial equilibrium and a sense of well-being. Needless to say, this behavior may be illegal, immoral and, in the long run, may even constitute an act against self-interest. But this is not always the case where altruistic acts against self-preservation interests are in conscious control of the decision-making brain circuitry. There have been recently published fMRI studies on decision-making choices of alternatives demonstrating the individualized nature of these processes where ongoing, real-time experiences seem to counter well thought analytical conclusions in the subjects tested. If the experience and peremptory satisfaction of a sense of biopsychosocial well-being controls our existential reality, then what can we say about the prophets that, living under similar or worse existential circumstances before the influence of organized religions, were able to overcome those strong neuro-humoral emotional satisfaction drives and do the right thing where self-interest was not in exclusive control of behavior? What guided their sacrificial behavior against self-interest? There is definitely more to come on this issue. The living human species, and to a large extent other subhuman species, share a wide spectrum of properties and phenomena that are entirely absent from inanimate matter. Living organisms undergo metabolic activity, grow and differentiate, respond to sensory stimulation, move, develop complex, organized functional structures, show the results of inherited environmental fluctuations, reproduce, and die. They also develop significant ecological adaptive fitness to changing environments. This is the kind of behavior that a complex program can make a robot to perform without the choice of deciding not to comply as a conscious will. Can the rationalized metaphor of the epistemological human abstraction be separated from the circumstantial, ontological human of our historical experience? Quare. This is precisely what we find in controlled and falsifiable studies. The physical aspects of biological lives involves not only the replication of the nucleic acids that carry the genetic information, the memetic/epigenetic growth and maturation of the organism through a sequence of developmental steps that, exclusively in the case of humans, includes the ability to introspectively discover his individualized identity as distinct from others' and the surroundings. The discovery of self co-evolves with the faculty of a language faculty now able to represent existential reality as metaphors which most likely share an embodiment with other vital neuronal networks in the brain real estate. Like other animals, inherited and environmentally-acquired servo controls guide the genetic and epigenetic preservation of biological life and its relevant neuro-humoral concomitants. Unlike other animals, humans, in addition, rely on their unique ability of being conscious of self and others and evolve the language faculty for communication with self and others in creating a safe and progressive social environment fit for reproductive and creative social conviviality. Is the mind's conscious linguistic representation of existential reality as conceptual metaphor abstractions separate from the quotidian unconscious/subconscious servo control of behavior? Can the physical sense-phenomenal, perceptual data bases and their metaphysical metaphor representations thereof both instantiated/embodied and share common neuronal networks? If so, which one is in control in the decision-making process? Quare . . . it all depends. If we depend on recorded history, we would have to conclude that by and large experiencing the satisfaction of an adapted biopsychosocial equilibrated well-being at the very moment when a decision must be made will trump any other logically based abstraction or altruistic motive. Only by exception will anyone negate the exemplary lives of historical prophets to be guided by the larger, transcendental view of the metaphor abstraction coded by the language faculty; many times performing conscious altruistic acts contrary to self interests. Why so? Are they aliens from another galaxy, immune from the pains and tribulations of existential reality or are they privy to extrasensory guidance information, e.g., revelations? Lakoff, in his seminal work on 'Embodied cognition' 1963, in open defiance of Chomskian language dogma that grammar was independent of meaning, had already considered the idea that the mind is not only represented in the brain, but that the physical brain is causally efficient in controlling the metaphysical mind and not the other way around! Except in the cases of the historical prophets. However, counter-intuitive as it may sound, it is a self-evident fact of life for the majority of us mortals. To our knowledge, nobody has even tried to understand the details of this neuronal network instantiation /embodiment of language representations as universals, as metaphor or virtual reflections on existential reality. Thus, to understand the meaning of life and consciousness (not robotic awareness) we must cross disciplines, both the ontological perceptual of the natural physical sciences and the epistemological conceptual of metaphysical logic and adopt a hybrid epistemontological approach because our cognition of life and existence, that precedes every decision-making act, is influenced, if not determined, by our individualized experiences in the real time physical world. In my opinion there may have been a basic grammar structure, a la Chomsky, that enable communication to satisfy early basic childhood needs and then became the subject of a continuous evolution guided by psycho-social adaptive strategies, a type of generative semantics where much of our language structure derives from physical environmental interactions during the first few years of life. Lakoff and Johnson's 'Metaphors We Live By' can explain it better. What else can one say about existence?

In case you did not notice, which I doubt, this is an embellished, fictionalized account of my real-time experiences, as I would like people to remember me and not necessarily as they were, especially if it would reveal unintentional bad behavior as driven by circumstances not entirely within my control. We are not perfect and largely a creature of circumstances largely outside our abilities to effectively influence. But those circumstances we can still impact and change in a positive way. We have the moral obligation to become the agents of change according to our capacities to do so. If you are able to, and consciously would not, then you are living at the level of subhuman species, not better than your nice dog. If you enjoy that robotic enslavement, so be it and God bless you just the same.

CHAPTER 16

I think that sacrifice is inherent to love and care for others than self. Both Suzi and I loved our pets and each other, and the existential sacrifices all concerned were willing to make in the conclusion of our marital relationship was not necessarily inconsistent with their nobility and Christian values. I was grieving and hurting badly. While planning to pick up my daughters coming for a weekend visit I confessed to my then-estranged wife Suzi that I still loved her and want her to reconsider her plans of moving back home to Virginia. It is abundantly clear that in Suzi's mind, I had abandoned her for another escape into intellectual dreaming, the result of being overwhelmed by our many family issues. Suzi suggests that her remorse is due to my escapes into conceptual reality where nobody is hurt. She is sacrificial and has no time and space to think, the die is cast. This rift has caused major problems and has triggered the typical insecurity angst and rebellion qualia of the 60's generation amongst my 3 surviving daughters and son in dire need for valuable time to resolve their own health and potential unemployment worries. But Suzi was determined to give in into what she thought was her destiny, with total un-intended disregard for everything that was left behind, a broken home, pets and teary me. Once again, I relied on my careful handling of our past relationship after my first wife died and was able to feel there was nothing I could do to reverse the recent events. I also deliberately got distracted away with my perambulations in search for an understanding of life and consciousness, the same search I had now extended to include me and the behavior that may have caused this rift. I decided then to take my visiting daughters back to Maryland. So, we drove north and stopped at Virginia asking my daughters to continue home that I would join after a brief sojourn, again searching for answers for that mysterious self-annihilating behavior of Suzi, curiosity and love are a disease. So, they dropped me at the outer banks at a friendly bed-and-breakfast joint for the weekend while Suzy was hopefully resting at her lifetime friend Carol's home, a few miles away. The motel I was staying was your typical rustic, romantic abode, right on the beach, where the North Atlantic wavelets traveled to the surf at high tide. I was one of many guests for that long holiday weekend. There was me, pitiful Yogi, a very antisocial, un-engaging TYPE A personality neuroscientist arriving at the inn with my own charged emotional baggage. I couldn't hold back the unending trail of flashbacks about my dear Labrador-chow Charlie Boy and the Memaw cats, I was then sure Miss Kitty, the feral cat, was already dead trying to find her way back to her native Deltona, Florida. God knows, I may one day greet her back at the shores of Lake Louise in Deltona. Above all I kept thinking about Suzi sitting near the table surrounded by her breathing equipment struggling to breathe, looking for a pack of menthol lights cigarettes within her addictive sight. I couldn't hold back my tears in front of the bar tender who lifted his eyes momentarily as he poured some Michelob dark beer inside my tall 12 ounce glass while I avoided direct eye contact by swinging my tall chair towards the stormy ocean landscape. I was beginning to wonder how I could possibly call her on the phone. I had no car and the weather was turning ugly, a storm was moving in. But I was on a mission. I picked up my unpredictable cell phone and nervously dialed her number, hoping she still owned the same one she had when she disappeared forever from my life. I got a response, as if she had been waiting for my call. My heart was beating fast and I walked outside so I could hear better. The wind was beginning to sing like Charlie-Boy's howling dog sounds. After a brief exchange of pleasantries, I told her where I was staying and without thinking, typical Suzi, she said "wait for me, I'll be there soon in a blue car, I'll honk twice when I arrive." Before I could reply she hung up saying "I love you". That was my Suzi alright.

There she is now arriving in a blue Chevy. You could always trust her determination. I was awakened from my brief mental trip by virtual Chevy, the black cat that stayed in Deltona, still helplessly looking for his Suzi, and by two loud honks from the car. I ran to the car to open her door, like in the good old times, I could not contain my tears again! What a curse to erupt my inner feelings like a volcano without a control! But, I didn't care, she was used to this embarrassing spectacle. I hugged her, put my arm around her shoulder and walked her back into the motel. I could feel with my finger the cloth texture of a familiar dress. Of course, it was the unforgettable white linen dress I was attracted to when I first met her at Hospice when grieving for our respective dead spouses. We walked in to a table overlooking the graying Atlantic Ocean as she would have expected and probably predicted for a Piscean like me. We dined together, sipped red Cabernet Sauvignon as I watched every muscle of expression on her face as she knew I would be doing, trying to read what's in her subconscious mind before she told me. She was beautiful to my biased eyes and nervous as usual. Several naturally aging white hairs were cascading down to her darkened eyebrows covering the also natural signs of frontal fissures. We shared trivial recent short stories before eventually turning nervously to each other as if pleading for emotional comfort. Almost as if a genuine first sight romance had been reborn. I opened up, at every moment praying that my calm, slow and good- mannered views on things would not be misconstrued as if preaching and/or criticizing. This was her standard misconception of viewing me, the typical retired professor, -ex-cathedra-, as always riding up in a tall high horse, as if ready to pass judgments on her nervous demeanor and experiences. Far from it. As always, I always felt guilt and regretted passing up a typical fatherly relationship with my beautiful family of 3 sons and 2 daughters in favor of a busy professional career as a university professor, a practicing medical malpractice lawyer and now—upon retirement—as a make believe neurophilosopher workaholic in training. I tried real hard to project into Suzi my premonition of seeing her struggling, for what likely will be unbearable days of grief and suffering dictated by her chronic obstructive respiratory condition and her negative family experiences. She looked to me in sadness as she nervously clenched her ever-present pack of menthol light cigarettes. At the same time, I was trying very hard to convince her of -somehow slowly- approaching her direct family until the -eventually wiser and more mature others- provide a turning point in their relationship, allowing her to begin to deal with her anticipated COPD Via Crucis. She can always become the protagonist of that wisdom she is capable of and teach them by example her own special living story of a very special type of love, and encouraging them to seek that out for themselves in a not so distant future, someday when she will become history. But she was not really listening to me and I was not sure this attention deficit was intentional. Anyway, it was time for me to stop preaching and start listening to her familiar side of the story. After realizing she was not really telling me anything I had not heard robotically repeated before, I waited patiently and then suggested a walk outside. I was not making my point across what nature and circumstances imposed as a barrier. Why God?, I asked in silence. Taking, hand in hand, that quiet sojourn along the grayish and humid beach seascape was a respite from Suzi's heart-rending subconscious script. How sad, I complained to my God; why do you do that to her . . . . and to me? She projected a long look that could have reached outer space in search of something unknown. I also searched in vain for any sign of

Antares, looking in vain for the constellation Scorpio where my mother, my uncle and my two older sons patiently await for me with open arms. Suddenly we were both synchronized on the famous painting of the beach dancers on top of our chimney back in Florida. She held my hand and we danced on the beach sand as I held her tight to my chest when she cried and walked to the blue car. I followed her and opened the car door for her. She was teary and hesitant, and Suzi was finally able to kiss me goodbye. I watched the car speed away into the paved road heading back to what I prayed would be her final abode of health, happiness and social acceptance. Goodbye my love, I am sorry….

CHAPTER

I couldn't help thinking about Suzi as I slowly drove back to Deltona trying to avoid the flood patches along the North Carolina 'High' Bank's road. Hurricane Florence -now just a tropical depression- still threatened to submerge the lower banks of the High Banks! My tears and recent glaucoma laser-trabeculoplasty eye intervention were making my return home difficult and, as usual, I had to avoid this other hell by escaping into the comfort of a virtual reality trip and trying to keep my modern leased Nissan trajectory inside my right lane. Suzi reminded me of my female friends at Debary's VFW Post 8063, also engaged, like so many political others -like Commissioner Erika- to gain the respect and approval of many spoiled, macho-like "Sugar Daddy" males everywhere in contemporary sight. All of them Jeanne, Doris, Bonk, Jannette, Karin, etc. were never -allegedly- trying to control the social decision-making process or become "Sugar Mommy" females, only emulate -quite successfully- the "MeToo" civic/political movement among contemporary others. There was no doubt that, whereas the sugar in the daddy for men consisted of their physical health superiority, independence and economic resources and confined reality perspective, all the ladies had to do was patiently wait for the aging process to evolve into the future to see all those features work against males whose bad health, dependence, and defective family resources management narrow existential reality perspective and language acuity diminished their leadership when compared to their spouses/partner's now. This 'not so new' female existential superiority has been made obvious by recent technological advances and an increase of female access to higher education. These evolutionary progression in a constantly changing environment have been anticipated and discussed in various of my publications. No doubt that the biopsychosocial endowment of females will eventually control life in the mesoscopic upcoming reality because there is -and will be- more 'sugar in their mommys' as history has shown. Let us briefly examine this assertion as a concluding remark.

The quest for finding the all-encompassing, final theory of everything in reality (TOE) continues un-abated. The front runners' current effort seems to be resting on the premise that the final TOE must exclusively be a "coherent theoretical framework of physics" linking all aspects of the universe we all witness. Consequently, models of general relativity and quantum field theories lead the pack by successfully having both been modified, under a "Grand Unified Theory", to include all dimensions, from the unreachable cosmic infinities to the invisible subatomic manifolds, including particles unit mass and distances from each other. The interactions between these particles unified both leading approaches when it considered three non-gravitational forces, the "weak", "strong" and "electromagnetic" influences. What seems to be missing from this materialistic physicalist model?

At first sight, the "Grand Unified Theory" seems to deny or ignore the constant change all human observers experience as a function of time passed. In so doing this physical model naively believes their TOE model will become a truthful 'destination' instead of the necessarily incomplete 'journey' through time that it must be as environmental and other relevant circumstances evolve. What is most amazing is ignoring the inconceivable fundamental need for maintenance of life and a nervous system which must be part and parcel of any Theory of Everything. Rationality analysis is not superior to the emotionality equivalent of feelings because the latter is far more complex to ontologically describe or epistemologically explain, even with the assistance of mathematical logic. There is no complete model that can possibly exclude the narrator of any model. Life must be included, its regulation, biology, etc. The conscious configuration of the physical world is inextricably correlated to the Platonic world, as Roger Penrose suggested…and, if I may add, to the constantly evolving sophistication of female participation in our vital biosphere. Why? Because -if we ignore the probability of relevant/appropriate male genetic mutations as a function of time and the equivalent drastic change in the environmental milieu- women have comparatively more sugar in their Mommy's!

In summary, a biopsychosocial approach, including both the macro general relativity and the micro quantum fields physical model, makes it more complete and as such, better describes how to become better human beings with an improved knowledge of our needs and that of others sharing our ecological niche. It is true that the current formulation of general relativity and quantum field represent dimensional extremes of our experience of reality required unification but it is also incomplete in that it pays no attention to the undeniable influential role played by the observer-narrator/recorder of observed or measured events. A balanced view should include all biopsychosocial features, the biological nervous system, a sine qua non condition to have a self-conscious psychological mind, individualized and collective social activity to guaranty the survival of the human species. No brain, no self- conscious effort to reunite the required biopsychosocial and theosophical elements.

https://video.search.yahoo.com/search/video;_ylt=A0LEVwuyyWZao6QA1BxXNyoA;_ylu=X3oDMTEyNzVrY2ZyBGNvbG8DYmYxBHBvcwMxBHZ0aWQDQjQ0ODNfMQRzZWMDc2M-?p=toe+theory+of+everything&fr=yset_chr_cnewtab

Printed in the United States
By Bookmasters